BALKAN ECHO

by

G.G. Vandagriff

CHAPTER ONE

Evanston, Illinois

The hidden man watched Meredith Montgomery unlock her door in the light of the porch lantern. Her hair glowed a lustrous dark red. But she had been digging in dangerous places, opening old wounds. His past must remain buried. He had spent too many years and too much money closing graves and silencing storytellers to allow her to interfere.

If she exposed him, the charade that was his life would shatter into a million pieces.

But he knew how to wait. She had been very useful to him so far, helping him to locate the boy. Now, if she could just lead him to the boy's mother. He fingered the knife in his pocket, his old and silent friend.

* * *

Meredith tried to shake the feeling that she was being watched. She ran up the stairs, unlocked her three locks, and entered her condo. Throwing the deadbolt fast, she leaned against the door, taking a deep, shaky breath. The blinds were all down, so she didn't hesitate to flip the switches beside her, flooding the rooms with light—the parlor on the left, the dining room on the right, straight on through to the large living space she had created with her remodel.

She put her briefcase on the narrow table that ran across the back of the couch, took off her coat, and hung it in the closet.

He's out there. I know he's out there.

She wished Paula were here. Her former roommate was incredibly brave. Unfortunately for Meredith, she was now on her honeymoon in the Caribbean.

Once she had changed into jeans and a Fair Isle sweater, she tried to eat some crackers and brie, while watching the shaded windows for shadows. She was very glad she had followed David's suggestion to install motion-sensing lights outside. He didn't want Paula living in a house that wasn't well protected. His fiancé's ordeal last year had left him a bit jumpy.

Her phone rang in the pocket of her jeans. With dread, she drew it out and looked at the number. It was blocked. After a moment she answered.

She heard the Darth Vader-like breathing again. She knew it was only the sound of a voice-altering filter, and the man said nothing this time. After fifteen seconds of her unanswered "hellos," the caller hung up.

Trembling and clammy, she wished Aubrey were with her. She couldn't eat.

After a moment of scanning her kitchen, she grabbed her butcher knife, walked upstairs, and went into the bathroom and locked the door. Sitting on the closed toilet, she gripped her hands together around the knife.

Meredith had worked on exposés before, but never one that was as potentially explosive as this one. She was on the verge of uncovering things long buried.

If you can't stand the heat, get out of the kitchen. Investigative journalism isn't for wimps.

But it was her way of righting the world's injustices. She wasn't a cop or an FBI agent. Her weapon was the TV broadcast.

Meredith decided what she needed was a hot bath. She had a perfect Victorian tub—deep, long, and claw-footed. As she ran the water, she poured in lavender bath salts. While the aroma began to calm her, she undressed. Putting her long red hair up in a turbaned towel, she stepped into the tub.

Scalding water burned her feet. She climbed out instantly, hopping around on the cold tiles. Meredith pulled the plug on her tub and turned the water to cold. Sticking one foot at a time under the cold water, she felt some relief.

The tub needed scouring. Her phone was ringing in the pocket of her pants. By the time she got to it, the caller had hung up. Checking the number, she realized it was Aubrey.

Great. The one person I want *to call me.*

She called him back.

"Sorry," she said when he answered. "I couldn't get to the phone."

"That's all right. Just wanted to know if you were okay."

"I'm not. We need to get out of town. I know he was out there when I got home tonight."

"Do you want me to come over?"

She wanted it more than anything.

She dried her feet as she talked, trying to sound businesslike. "I'm trying to keep busy. I'll be fine. The door's locked."

"You going to scrub the tub?" he asked.

Now that's downright eerie.

"How did you know?"

"I could hear it draining in the background, and I'm well acquainted with your OCD."

"Now you've made my night. Remind me not to phone you back next time." She disconnected the call. She had no defenses left against this man. And she was going to be traveling to the deepest, darkest Balkans with him. Was she nuts?

She got out the cleanser and tackled the tub.

CHAPTER TWO

A week earlier

"There's a tipster on line two," Meredith's admin, Gwen, told her.

"A crackpot?" she asked.

"I can't tell. It could be something you want to look into. Sounds like he's done his research on you."

Meredith took the call.

"Ms. Montgomery?"

"This is she."

"I have just found out some alarming information the public should know."

"Why should the public know?" she asked, offering her standard response to this gambit.

"Because justice should be served."

"Justice or revenge?" she asked, trying to picture her caller. He had a deep voice and a slight accent she thought was Slavic. Revenge was a common motive for anonymous tipsters.

There was a beat of silence. Then the caller resumed, "Do you want a war criminal living in your country? A man guilty of genocide? This person is a sociopath. He has no conscience. He is a ticking time bomb."

"How do you know this?" Meredith asked, her heart speeding up.

"I witnessed the 'ethnic cleansing,' as they called it, in 1992. In Bosnia. I saw him committing unspeakable acts."

She sat up straighter, trying to rein in her interest. "Surely there is a protocol in place for dealing with such a man."

"I know what I say to be true, but it will have to be proven. I know that, for an American, you are an expert on the Balkans. I know you are also one of the best investigative journalists in the country . . ."

"You can skip the flattery," she said. "What is this man's name?"

"His name is Zoran Duric. I saw him on the street in Chicago. He was on Michigan Avenue. I think he works at the Mercantile Exchange."

"That's a Serbian name. Are you Muslim or Croatian?"

"As a matter of fact, I consider myself a Bosnian of Serbian descent. I know what the world thinks of us, but not all Serbs betray their own people the way this man has done."

"So, you just saw him on a Chicago street? And you recognized him after twenty-five years?"

"He has a face you don't forget."

"And you won't tell me your name?"

"I'm not stupid. I realize this isn't cut and dried, but you're a journalist. I know your work. You always do a lot of research. If you capture Duric, you will make the world a safer place."

"I hardly think the man is still committing genocide," said Meredith, wincing. She sounded like a scoffer. She didn't like scoffers.

"I have heard rumors that he still visits Bosnia. And surely you know that unexplained deaths still occur," her informant insisted.

"That sounds very nebulous."

The man's tone switched from insistent to businesslike. "If you follow this up, you will be doing a service to mankind. Isn't that why you became a journalist?"

Meredith felt a twinge of guilt. Of course, the man was right.

"I'll do some background research. There were a lot of war crimes committed during that time. Can you be more specific?"

"He was one of the conspirators who kidnapped the Muslim leader, Izetbegovic, from Sarajevo and held him hostage. But the worst crimes he committed were in Zvornik, along the Bosnian border with Serbia during the spring and summer of 1992, when they were trying to clear out the Croats and the Muslims. They wanted to create a Serbian zone inside Bosnia along the border with Serbia.

"They chose the worst kind of force. You know, of course, that the 'ethnic cleansing' was nothing but pure terrorism to get people to flee."

"I hadn't thought of it that way, but it makes a horrible kind of sense."

Genocide was genocide, even if it happened twenty-five years ago. In the midst of the modern-day bloodbath in the Middle East, could she even interest her boss in this?

She expressed this concern to her caller. Then she asked, "Where were you exactly? When? What did you see? Would you be willing to be quoted on an anonymous basis about what you saw? Do you have pictures?"

"I was in the Drina River Valley in May and July of 1992 where the First Krajina Corps of the Serbian rebel army committed some of the worst atrocities of the war. I could write out a statement for you to read. I do have pictures, but they are old and faded."

"I can only promise to bring this up with my boss. If he gives me the okay, I'll look into it. How can I get in touch with you?"

"You won't need that information to do your job." The caller disconnected.

Writing the name Zoran Duric on a fresh legal tablet, she put it aside and went back to a diet food fraud story she was working on.

But the name Zoran Duric and his alleged crimes would not fade from her mind. Unfortunately, she knew what those crimes would have entailed. That afternoon she called her college roommate, Allie.

"What's up, Meredith?" her friend answered.

"I need to ask you to do something for me. It's about a potential story. How about we have dinner tonight? Is that enough of a bribe?"

"It is if we go to O'Henry's."

"Okay. It's a deal. Seven o'clock?"

"See you, then. I'm in the middle of vaccinating a litter of puppies, so bye."

"Bye."

She decided she had researched her current story within an inch of its life, so she left it and went to talk to Aubrey in his cubicle about her anonymous tip.

As usual, he needed a haircut. His thick, light brown hair fell over his deep brown eyes. Unfortunately, Meredith found it a very attractive look. And, as she was nearly six feet, she liked that he was tall—six feet, six inches. (She had stolen a peek at his driver's license when he had his wallet open).

"What's up, Merry?" he asked.

"You know I hate that name."

"Yeah, I do. But you didn't answer my question."

"I had a call today. It got to me, but I'm not sure it should have." She gave him the details.

"Whoa," he said when she finished. "All that happened when we were about two. It's not exactly news."

"I know. But I studied it at Northwestern. The peace process was part of a Poli Sci class."

"Do you think the public would really be interested?"

She put her hands on her hips. "There's still a furor over Nazi war criminals, and they're in their nineties."

"So how do you plan to tackle this?"

Sensing his softening, she abandoned her warlike stance. "I have to get Mr. Q's okay first. It's going to take a lot of research. I might even have to go to Bosnia."

Aubrey perked up. She knew he loved foreign travel. "Do you need a cohort on this? Believe it or not, I know a little about the war."

"I admit, it makes me a little nervous." She gave him a playful punch. "I could use a big, strong man like you."

"Let's make it official then," he said. "Assign me a task."

She recognized the glint in his eye that he got when he was interested in a story.

"Come with me to see Mr. Q and help me convince him of the newsworthiness of my story. Then come to dinner with me tonight to meet my friend who is the daughter of a Bosnian."

"Done," he said.

Bald as an egg, Mr. Q had small eyes that sparkled when he got excited about a story. They didn't sparkle over this one.

"This does not qualify as 'news you can use,' Meredith."

"I have heard the Bosnian war described as a post-modern war," she said. "Certainly, it pre-figured modern-day terrorism."

"And that should interest me because . . ." he said.

She used her informant's words. "We have a sociopath living among us. He's a ticking time bomb. He uses terror as a means to an end. Who knows what will next set him off?"

"Especially with all the Muslim refugees moving to Chicago," Aubrey said. "They are his blood enemy."

Mr. Q arched his fingers. "That's an interesting approach. Okay. Put this down as priority number two to whatever else comes up."

When Meredith and Aubrey left the office, they high-fived one another. He followed her to her desk.

"So," she said. "How much do you know about the Bosnian war?"

"When Yugoslavia splintered after Tito died, all the ethnic groups got their own little country, except Bosnia. It had three ethnic groups: Serbians, Muslims leftover from the Ottoman Empire, and Croatians. They just sort of spontaneously combusted. The fighting was primitive and beyond brutal. The Americans thought it was just the Serbs who practiced genocide, but it wasn't only them. The Muslims and the Croats committed acts of 'ethnic cleansing' as well. The whole idea behind it was for each group to clear a place for a 'pure blood' people within Bosnia."

"How did you come to be well-informed?" she asked, almost breathless.

"I never reveal my sources."

"And the Dayton Peace Accords?" she asked.

"A work of political artistry, and impossible to sum up in a few words. They succeeded because everyone got part of what they wanted, but not everything they wanted. This solution prevented one party from thinking the other party won."

"One day I will torture you, and you will tell me how and why you know so much."

* * *

O'Henry's in Evanston was a womb-like Irish pub where Meredith had been hanging out since she was a student. They had a limited, but delicious menu of Irish favorites.

Allie awaited Meredith and Aubrey in a booth under an old Prohibition poster. She stood at their approach and hugged Meredith.

"Allie, meet Aubrey Kettering, a colleague from work. Aubrey, this is Allie Novak, my sorority sister and roommate."

The two shook hands.

"So, this is something to do with work?" Allie asked with a mischievous grin. "Are you investigating me?"

"No. I just want to ask you some questions. But let's eat first," said Meredith. "I missed lunch."

Meredith and Allie wanted their standard: fish and chips. Aubrey ordered corned beef hash.

Meredith opened her purse and took out the hand sanitizer. "Anyone?" she offered it around the table.

Aubrey laughed. "No thanks." But Allie accepted the offer. "I forgot to wash my hands when I left work."

"Ew," said Meredith.

"Get over it," said Allie.

While they were eating, Allie asked, "Where did you study, Aubrey? You already know we were here at Northwestern."

"I'm a University of Chicago undergrad. Crossed over to the dark side when I went to Medill for my masters at j-school, like Allie. Most of us from WOOT TV went to school together," he said.

"So what made you want to study journalism? Is it your way of standing for truth, justice, and the American way like Meredith?"

He laughed. "Pretty much. I specialize in subversive stuff."

"Otherwise known as hacking," said Meredith. "He's a genius at it."

"And how do you earn your bread?" Aubrey asked Allie, who Meredith acknowledged was very attractive to men with her curvy, petite figure.

"I'm a vet, which sometimes has its own kind of excitement." She exhibited a bandage on her arm.

"The puppies?" asked Meredith.

"No. A wounded Doberman. He was angry at the world, and I can't blame him. Someone took a shot at him."

"That's awful!" said Meredith.

"What would life be like without drama?" asked Allie.

When they had finished, and their plates were removed, Meredith asked, "Does your dad ever talk about the Bosnian War?"

"Never. Period," said Allie. "Why?"

Meredith told her about the odd phone call she had taken.

"Strange. Sounds like something out of a World War II thriller about the Nazis," said Allie. "How does he expect you to find a man he saw on the street?"

"I didn't ask, but I suspect he thinks I have magic powers."

"I don't want to rain on your parade," Allie said. "There's a reason why people have come here from Bosnia, but they haven't left their Bosnian grudges behind. The dead are remembered. Their deaths are unavenged. This guy wants you to avenge him. It could be awfully dangerous."

"That's why she has me," said Aubrey. "I'm her own personal Doberman."

"I wondered where you came into the picture," said Allie. "Have you been vaccinated for rabies?"

They all laughed.

Allie asked, "What is it you want to ask my Dad? If he's ever heard of this guy? Serbians and Croatians aren't exactly buddy-buddy, you know."

"Yeah, but both of them are Bosnian. They were there during the war, right?" Meredith asked. "And now they're both in Chicago. It's not too much of a stretch to think they might have at least heard of each other, right?"

"My dad is a complete recluse. You know that. I blame the war, and I really don't want to bring up some random Serb, unless you can't find him any other way. Did you know there are 30,000 Serbs living in Chicago? And that's down from 50,000 about twenty years ago."

Astounded, Meredith said, "I had no idea. Do you know if there is, like, a Bosnian enclave on the South or West Side somewhere? It seems they have every other nationality there."

"I think the Bosnian Serbs hang out with the Serbs from Serbia, the Bosnian Croats with the Croatians from Croatia," said Aubrey. "Who knows who the Muslims hang with? But I'll look into it."

"I'm sorry I can't help with my dad. That is such a bitter memory," said Allie. "Remember, Serbs killed my mom."

"I guess I'd forgotten that. Sorry to be so insensitive," Meredith said.

"No problem." Allie shrugged her shoulders. "It seems that these days everyone has to walk on eggshells to avoid offending someone else."

"I'm going to put my mouth in time out," said Meredith.

Aubrey chuckled. "That would be a novelty."

"Okay, Mr. Strong Silent Type. That's enough out of you," said Meredith, surprisingly hurt by his comment.

"Asking questions is what good journalists do," said Aubrey. "And you're a good journalist. You don't see me on the TV, breaking stories, do you? I'm staff. I do what I'm told."

"You're too modest," said Meredith, a tiny bit mollified. Did she really talk too much? How awful.

Because of that exchange, when Aubrey took her home later, she didn't invite him in for coffee as she'd planned.

CHAPTER THREE

Aubrey could have bitten his tongue for the caustic comment he had made about Meredith's mouth. It was a beautiful, Ingrid Bergman mouth. He had hurt her, and he didn't mean it as anything more than friendly ribbing. He was always doing stuff like that.

The fact was, being with Meredith made him nervous, which was strange because, for the most part, he was at his ease with women. Oh, well. Maybe he could make it up to her by the depth of his knowledge about their subject.

For as long as he could remember, he had followed his father's lead and hidden his mother's Serbian heritage. He had grown up privileged as the son of a professor at the University of Chicago, but he was still a product of the South Side. He knew plenty about the war, especially since his father had been a member of the U.N. peacekeeping force. And his mother had taught him Serbo-Croatian. When it was just the two of them, he spoke her language. He knew that all three of Bosnia's minorities were very well represented in Chicago.

He phoned his father during his office hours at the university the next day.

"Dad, I'm doing a story on a Serbian war criminal who has been seen on the streets of Chicago. Did you or mom ever hear of a guy named Zoran Duric?"

There was a long pause. "Where did you get his name?"

"An anonymous caller. He phoned the station to say he'd spotted him on the streets near the Mercantile Exchange. He wanted us to out him."

He heard his father sigh heavily. "Go softly, Aubrey. That fellow was a real butcher. We never caught him. He disappeared sometime after the war, so he wasn't prosecuted at the Hague. And don't bother your mother with questions. She's been having the nightmares again."

"Is she at home or back in the hospital?"

"She's trying to stay home this time. She hates the psych ward. If you visit, please don't talk about the war."

Aubrey felt guilty. He didn't visit his parents very much since he had become a Northsider. He told himself it was because he was always under a deadline.

"Okay. Maybe I'll go down there today. What can you tell me about Duric?"

"That you should not follow up on this. Report it to the FBI and let it go. He was the worst of the worst. You cannot imagine, Aubrey. Even in the midst of a horrible war, he was someone who stood out as pure evil. He really enjoyed killing. And he was a true racist. He hated the Muslims the way Hitler hated the Jews."

"Not the kind of guy we want loose in Chicago, then."

"Definitely not."

"Thanks, Dad. I really appreciate this."

"Follow my advice, son. Just this once. It won't be just him. He always has henchmen nearby."

* * *

Stopping to buy his mother a box of chocolate Frango Mints, Aubrey headed down Lake Shore Drive to the South Side. He loved driving along the lake with the top down on his Mustang on a nice late summer afternoon. The sailboats were out in force. Too bad David was in the Caribbean. There wouldn't be too many more days to go out with him in his boat before Chicago winter set in. Sometimes he felt like a figurative bear, stocking up on sun-filled experiences before hibernating.

Of course, he wouldn't follow his father's advice. And his father knew that he wouldn't. A good journalist went after the dangerous stories. There was also the fact that he needed to protect Meredith.

His mother was having tea when he arrived. Stana Kettering was a beautiful woman with a carefully maintained appearance. She highlighted her hair to cover the encroaching gray, she always had her nails manicured, and her make up on, even for a day at home.

She was overjoyed to see Aubrey, kissing him on both cheeks. "Oh, darling. You are so welcome! What brings you home in the middle of the day?"

"Dad said you were having the nightmares again."

Her face crumpled, and she turned away. "He should not have told you."

"He knew I would be concerned. What can I do to make things better for you? Would you like to take a drive along the lake shore? Maybe walk out on the pier?"

"Oh, Aubrey! That would be lovely."

"Bundle up," he said. "Fall is coming early. There is a breeze off the lake. It looks warmer than it is."

They walked out on Navy Pier, enjoying the sailboats together, his mother's arm through his.

"This wind will blow those terrible goblins right out of my head," she said.

"I hope so," said Aubrey. "And you know you mustn't feel guilty for having those nightmares. It's PTSD. Even the bravest soldiers suffer from it."

"Those lovely mints you brought me will give me only sweet dreams," she said, patting his hand.

He longed to ask her about her experiences, but he was frightened of deepening her depression. Aubrey had never known exactly what had happened to his mother. But there was also the promise he made to his father. He only wished there was some way he could lift her burden. At least, today seemed to be helping.

He talked to her about David and Paula's wedding, their honeymoon in the Caribbean, and the success of their last case.

"I am so glad for David that he has found this happiness," she said. "I have always been fond of him. And I must tell you, I did not like his first fiancée. Sherrie was too self-centered. She did not deserve him."

"I agree with you. I was not a big Sherrie fan."

"But were you sad, my dear? I know you dated Paula yourself. I liked her."

"For her, it was always David, and I knew it, even if he didn't catch on. I didn't really have a chance with her."

"Another woman will catch your eye."

He kept silent about Meredith. He had made the mistake of introducing his mother to Paula, spawning wild hopes on her part. Besides, he wasn't even certain if Meredith liked him never mind wanting to have a relationship with him. Plus relationships with co-workers were always a bit of a risk.

After their walk on the pier, he and his mother had coffee and talked about his father.

"He works too hard," she said, as she always did. "He has tenure, but he still works like he's afraid he'll be fired. And his students! They call and come by at any time, day or night."

"He's a great professor," said Aubrey. "He inspires devotion. It's rare to find a man like Dad when you're going through school. They're all probably looking for a father figure."

"He is a great man. That is why I married him. I really cannot blame the students, I guess."

Aubrey took his mother home and bade farewell to her, driving back downtown to try to catch Meredith before she left for the day.

* * *

"So," he said to Meredith as they went to one of the downtown bars after work. He noticed, not for the first time that she only drank cola. "There really *are* 30,000 Serbs in Chicago! More than in any other country except Serbia. They're down on the southeast side and live right near the Croatians—by choice, which is weird considering how much they hated each other twenty-five years ago. But Serbs outnumber the Croats by about five to one. Both groups have worked in the steel mills for generations. In case you didn't know, Serbs are Eastern Orthodox, Croatians are Catholic."

"What about the Muslims?"

"Now that's interesting. The Bosnian Muslims are far more uptown. Near North Side at first but now their main mosque is in Northbrook.

"The Arab Muslims have a whole different society in the south and southwest neighborhoods. They're mostly Palestinians. Far less prosperous than the Bosnian Muslims. I suspect the new immigrants are all going to join those neighborhoods. They certainly wouldn't fit in with the Bosnian Muslims."

"Interesting. Hmm," said Meredith. "Thank you for researching that. Very interesting about the two different groups of Muslims."

"I have a confession to make," he said.

"You are secretly married," she said, perfectly straight-faced.

"Not quite. But my dad was a U.N. Peacekeeper in Bosnia. It sounds like I spent the afternoon researching when I really went for a walk on Navy Pier with my mom." He studied his hands and then looked up at her through his lashes. Her eyebrows were arched in surprise. He continued, "My dad has taught me a lot about the war in Bosnia and its minorities over the years. He's a professor of Political Science concentrating on central and eastern Europe."

"Dr. Kettering! Wow! I should have put the two of you together. It's not that common a name." Her eyes were bright with excitement. "You should be a great asset on this story. Maybe you should take it over. It sounds like it's in your blood."

More than you know.

CHAPTER FOUR

"I asked my father if he knew of Zoran Duric," Aubrey said.

He sounded so solemn suddenly. She studied his face. "And?"

"He begged me not to proceed with the investigation. He said Duric was a real butcher. He was very concerned. According to him, Duric hated the Muslims like Hitler hated the Jews."

"So, it sounds like he knew details," Meredith said, elated. "We have to interview him, Aubrey. We need to know just how bad Duric is."

Her friend was quiet. He took a swig of his bourbon. Turning to face her, he said, "I'm not sure you really understand what type of man this guy is. If my *dad* called him a butcher, he was guilty of horrendous crimes. He won't want to be found, and if he knows someone is looking, he won't hesitate to snuff that someone out. I got the impression he has a hair trigger. I don't have to tell you that he's a killer and there are plenty more killers who would kill him."

Meredith contemplated his words. Was she willing to risk her life for her career? She shivered. "He must be one really bad character."

"My dad wants us to hand this over to the FBI and let it alone."

"Do you think they would believe an anonymous tip about crimes committed twenty-five years ago?" she asked, well and truly sobered.

"Probably not high on their priority list."

"I suppose we could try it," she said. "I'll go in myself tomorrow morning." She looked it up on her phone. "Roosevelt Road. Right."

"I'll come with you. My dad's name might carry some weight since he was with the U.N."

"Thanks," she said and slipped off her stool. "I'd better be getting home."

"You taking the train?"

"Yes."

"I am, too. I'll come with you."

As they walked to the train, over the bridge, and across the river, Meredith felt his hand on her back through her coat as he ushered her through the crowds. Fall was coming, and the breeze off the river was cool. She was glad when they reached the warm train.

As they sat together, he said, "We can still talk to my father if you like. I think we should hear what he has to say."

"I confess I'm pretty curious."

"It's not going to be a pretty story, Meredith."

"I am not in search of a happy ending, for Pete's sake. Remember I studied the war."

"But you were in the ivory tower while you did so. My dad was 'boots on the ground.'"

His patronizing tone irritated her. "Don't assume you know everything about me," Meredith said, drawing herself away from him and shrinking together inside her coat. She found a vial of hand sanitizer in her pocket and, taking it out, she applied it and scrubbed her hands together. Trains had so many germs.

When they reached Evanston, Aubrey insisted on walking her to her condo. Again, she was irritated enough with him not to invite him in. "I'll pick you up at eight tomorrow morning," she told him.

* * *

She assembled the ingredients for a fruit and spinach smoothie after she had changed into jeans. When it was ready, she took it into the spare bedroom she had outfitted as a den. Out of the file cabinet, she took a fat file of letters that were all she had left of her father.

Meredith felt the sharp jab of grief that visited her so often since he had died of an unexpected stroke last summer. She had been abroad, interviewing Middle Eastern refugees, and had not even been able to say good-bye.

She forced herself to sip at the smoothie she didn't want. She had lost entirely too much weight, and as tall as she was, she couldn't afford it. The svelte Audrey Hepburn was decades out of date. J-Lo was in.

She held the letters to her chest, and gradually she felt a warmth there.

Dear Dad. What would you do in my shoes? Would you go ahead with the investigation?

She knew that he would. His news stories had had all the immediacy of an eye-witness. He had traveled around the world to do his job on location. Few of her current friends knew that her father was William Montgomery, a Pulitzer Prize-winning Foreign Correspondent for CNN. He had covered the Bosnian War and written a book about it: *The Broken Crystal*.

They had used his book in her class on the Dayton Peace Accords. But she had something over and above that. Opening her file, she found the letters to her mother from 1992-93.

She knew them well, but the Slavic names had never really registered because unsure how to pronounce them, she had skipped over all but the most important ones. Now she looked for any mention of Zoran Duric.

Since he had corresponded weekly, she had many letters to look through. Fortunately, the missives were typed and easy to read. She skimmed for half an hour, her smoothie gone until she found a single mention:

The worst of these evil men is Zoran Duric. I have made it my mission to take recorded statements of his atrocities. My photographer has captured the results of his rampages through the settlements along the river that borders Serbia. The massacre at Zvornik was horrific. I am certain there will be a War Tribunal at some point, and I plan to submit my evidence.

Meredith wondered if her father had, in fact, carried through. Putting all the letters back together, carefully filing them by date, she went to the file drawer for a document she had read for her class on the break-up of the former Yugoslavia. It was a White Paper compiled by the University of Dayton on the criminals not yet prosecuted by the Hague and those that had been.

Sure enough, Zoran Duric was one of those listed as "at large" at the end of the war. His crimes were many, but his death was reported at the hands of Bosnian Muslims in Sarajevo in 1995. She double checked the facts on Google. The source for the Wikipedia entry on Duric was the same University of Dayton White Paper she had read. Was he really dead? Had her anonymous caller been seeing ghosts? For a moment, she knew doubt. Maybe his death had been staged—a charade. She knew the Hague Tribunal had lasted twenty-four years, ending only a year ago. If she could prove the man was alive, would his sentence be carried out? She must ask Dr. Kettering.

What would her father want her to do? Surely, if he were alive and had received the anonymous call, he would have followed through on it. He would have done everything he could to bring the notorious man to justice if he was indeed alive.

But how would he feel about *her* being that instrument of justice? Dad had harbored a very high opinion of her scholarship and her efforts as an investigative journalist, but, after all, he had seen of the world, he was very protective of her, as well.

At that moment, her phone rang. Meredith sprang up from her position on the floor where she had been reading and answered.

The first thing she heard was breathing—mechanical breathing like Darth Vader in Star Wars. She was about to hang up when she heard the words, "Zoran Duric is dead. He died in Sarajevo years ago at the hands of Muslim terrorists. You may cease your investigation now."

The call ended. Meredith felt clammy and shaken. For a moment she just stood, focusing on the streetlamp outside her window without seeing it. She sank into her loveseat.

The voice had been the eeriest thing she'd ever heard. Of course, it was only one of those devices used by people who wanted to distort their voices. But it made her feel violated, made her feel as though her condo were a foreign place.

Her instinct told her to call her father. A hole wrenched open inside her as though she had been stabbed repeatedly. Her father was gone.

I have to do something. Going to the kitchen, she grabbed a spray can of Lysol and found a clean rag. She sprayed the rag with the disinfectant and scrubbed every inch of her phone.

Aubrey. I must get to Aubrey.

The only weapon she had was an old police baton Paula had given her from a police auction she had attended.

Not waiting even to warn him she was coming, she grabbed her coat and hat, locked all three of her locks behind her, and got into her vintage Mustang. Fortunately, Aubrey only lived in Skokie, one suburb west.

When she pulled up beside his condo, she was still shaking. Some heroine she was! She rushed up the stairs and pounded on the door of his walk-up.

When he answered, she could hear a Rachmaninoff piano concerto banging through the room behind him.

"Do you have a gun?" she asked.

"Meredith, you're dead white. What's wrong? Is someone after you?"

"I've had a scare," she said. "May I come in?"

"Yes, yes, of course. Let me just turn that down. Can I take your coat?"

"No. I need it," she said. "Do you have a gun?" she asked again.

"As a matter of fact, I do. Why? Am I going to need it?"

"I hope not," she said. "Someone knows what we're doing. Someone called me and was all Darth Vadery. You know—voice altering equipment. He said Zoran Duric was dead. Killed years ago in Sarajevo by Muslims. How did he know what we're doing?"

"I have no idea. But obviously, someone's trying to head us off," Aubrey said. "I'm sorry you're so frightened. Let me get you some brandy."

"No. No liquor," she said. "C-could you just sit close to me, and maybe put your arm around me?"

Looking surprised, Aubrey led her to his living room. His sound system with different varieties of speakers mounted on his walls dominated the room. He had a black leather couch where she sat. He pulled her to him and spoke into her hair. "A kid can speak into one of those things and scare the liver out of anyone. He's trying to throw us off. I don't believe him."

"Th-the odd th-thing was I had just read that information in a White Paper. I was ready to give up. B-but now I think the report is bogus."

"The clown miscalculated badly."

"Do you know how to shoot?" she asked.

"Of course."

"I learned to shoot when I was in the Mideast. I'm going to buy a gun. I felt so un-unsafe."

"Meredith, this is totally unlike you. What is wrong?"

She could never tell him the horrors she had passed through, why that harsh voice had freaked her out so badly.

"If you won't take liquor, I'm going with hot milk. My mom's cure for nightmares. She knows what she's doing, too. Come with me to the kitchen?"

Meredith let herself be charmed by the technical wonder of Aubrey's kitchen. He had every device money could buy. All the appliances were stainless and up to the minute. "I didn't know you could cook."

"It's my stress-release. He poured a glass of whole milk into a white pottery latte cup and set it in the microwave to heat. When a minute and twenty seconds had passed, he stirred in a tablespoon of honey and sprinkled the top of the concoction with nutmeg.

"Here. It'll work wonders, I promise you."

She carried it back into the living room. "Can you play *The Moonlight Sonata*?" she asked.

"Anything to help," he said. He fiddled with his phone, and soon the familiar music came on.

He sat back next to her on the couch. "Talk to me, Meredith. Why are you so scared?"

"I can't. I can't bring it to the surface, or I won't be able to function. This milk will help. Thanks."

"You've got my bed tonight. I'll sleep out here."

She didn't even protest, except to say, "Thank you. I'll change the sheets myself. Don't worry about it."

"Of course, you will," he said with a laugh. "I wasn't worried at all."

* * *

She rose before Aubrey was up and felt like the girl who had cried wolf. She put her sheets in the washer and, sneaking into the kitchen she wrote a note, "Sorry for the drama. Have gone home to change. Will still pick you up at eight. Thanks. MM.

On the drive back home, she chastised herself. Aubrey would never look at her the same. His image of her would be forever tainted by the gibbering idiot she had been last night. In the long run, maybe that was best. She wouldn't get involved with anyone again. Ever.

Determined to change her appearance, she wore her most conservative ensemble—a black pantsuit with a cream blouse—and put her red hair in a bun at the nape of her neck. She studied her features as she put on her makeup. Gray-blue eyes seemed overly large in her thin face. Her cheekbones were so sharp they could have cut bread. Thank heavens for braces and straight teeth. Hers had been a mess.

Her experience with e. Coli in Africa last spring had taken its toll. She should have come home after that. But she was so determined to prove how tough she was she had gone on to the Middle East to finish her story on refugees. Of course, she had wanted to accompany Jan... But she wouldn't allow herself to think of that.

That was where she had been when she heard of her father's death. The news had finished her. Everyone thought she was still in Africa, but she had come back to the states and gone to her parents' cabin on Michigan's Upper Peninsula where she had done nothing but sleep for a month. Dad had been her soul mate in so many ways. She had to keep reminding herself she was not alone and that her work was still worth doing. But she knew she was finished with love.

Swamped in her own grief, Meredith's mother had not been able to reach out as much as she might have. But she loved Meredith as unconditionally as it was possible for a parent to do. That love was the only thing that had kept Meredith from plunging to the bottom. She had called her mom from Michigan after two weeks, and the new widow had joined her at the cabin. They had grieved together.

Her roommate, Paula, had been fond of telling her that most people weren't as lucky as she was in the parent department. Her friend had had a sad year, and her losses had not been easy either. But she had carried on, fueled by a desire for justice.

Was that why Meredith was so anxious to take on this Zoran Duric's capture?

Meredith left to pick Aubrey up at his condo for their visit to the FBI.

"Are you looking to get hired?" he asked. "You look just like an agent in that black suit with your hair that way."

She smiled. "Is your Dad okay with us visiting him this afternoon?"

"Yeah. He's cleared an hour for us. One to two."

On the way to the FBI, she told him about her research on Duric.

"He sounds like a desperate character. But maybe he *is* dead. Maybe your original informant was seeing things. You know—PTSD or something."

"But why would someone call and scare me to death, warning me off if there wasn't something to find? This stinks, Aubrey."

"Well, we'll see what the FBI has to say about it all."

Meredith was taken aback by the sight of the modern FBI headquarters. It was a many-storied modern glass and steel building. More glass than steel. Not at all what she had expected.

"Our tax dollars at work," said Aubrey. "I had something from the Work Projects Administration in mind."

"Me, too," she said.

A no-nonsense receptionist was ready to take their inquiry.

Meredith said, "I am Meredith Montgomery, and this is Aubrey Kettering. We're from WOOT TV. We want to report a possible sighting of a Bosnian war criminal. He is guilty of genocide."

"Oh! Well, I'll see if one of our assistant special agents-in-charge can meet with you. Please take a seat."

Twenty minutes later, a short, boxy man with intense blue eyes approached them, his hand outstretched. "Hamilton Werner. Sorry for the wait."

Aubrey introduced both of them. They handed him their business cards.

"But I understood this was about a war criminal. You're here for the TV station?"

"No," said Meredith. "We'll explain."

"Fine. There's a room up on the second floor where we can talk. I'll lead the way."

The room was all glass on one side and wood-paneled on the others with a forest green plush carpet. They sat at a long glass conference table.

Meredith told him about her anonymous call. She also told him about the White Paper's report of his committing genocide and its assertion that Duric had been killed by Muslims in Sarajevo. Haltingly, she told him of the anonymous phone call she had received the night before.

"So," said Werner. "Why did you feel compelled to bring this news to me? If the man is dead?"

"We want to follow up on the story," said Aubrey. "If Meredith's informant was telling the truth and was not mistaken, there is a dangerous sociopath living at large in Chicago. The man who called Ms. Montgomery last night meant to intimidate her into stopping her search."

"It *would* make a very good story," the assistant SAC said.

"When my father, Dr. Kettering down at University of Chicago, was a U.N. Peacekeeper, he knew of the man. He said he was the worst of the butchers," said Aubrey. "If anyone knew he was alive, there would be an international arrest warrant."

"And my father, who was a war correspondent in Bosnia, singled him out for the same reason. He even wrote home about him," said Meredith.

"Have you any idea of the amount of crime in Chicago?" Werner asked. "Of course you do. You're the press. Let's put it another way. How can we possibly justify the man-hours it would take to investigate the rumor about someone who committed crimes twenty-five years ago and who is probably dead?" Meredith felt foolish. "We do intend to investigate," she said. "But we didn't want to step on any toes."

The man passed a business card to each of them. "If it turns out he's alive and in Chicago, we would help to bring him in. Here's how you can get in touch with me."

She and Aubrey stood. Werner ushered them out of the room and all the way down in the elevator.

"Good hunting!" he said by way of farewell.

CHAPTER FIVE

Aubrey's father's office was pleasant and professorial looking. There was a Persian rug on the floor, large velvet-draped windows, oak-paneled walls, and a portrait of Thomas Jefferson.

As Aubrey and Meredith sat in brown leather chairs before a fire, he told his father about the assertions from two different sources that Duric was dead, and the FBI's response to the situation.

"I might have believed the university White Paper more if it hadn't been for the sci fi phone call. That was meant to frighten, to intimidate," Aubrey's father said. "The caller, if it was Duric, miscalculated badly. He always did go in for the grand gesture. He never made a secret of his crimes." He steepled his fingers. "Also, I am familiar with that White Paper. It was written by a professor's assistant and is poorly researched. The assertion that Duric was dead may have been rumor only. Rumor spread by Duric himself."

"The FBI will provide muscle if we can find the man," said Meredith. "Where would you start?"

"I am disappointed in their response. There are good reasons, which I am not at liberty to share with you, why the two of you must *not* be the ones searching for him. Leave this alone. Do a background piece, a color piece if you wish. The twenty-third anniversary of the Dayton Peace Accords is coming up. Concentrate on what a miracle it is that the document has for the most part halted a feud of truly Biblical proportions."

Aubrey felt like a deflated balloon. He had felt certain his father would be eager to help them. What were the things he wasn't at "liberty" to discuss? It wasn't like he was a spy or something. Was he just afraid of putting his own son in danger?

Seeming to read his thoughts, the professor said, "Believe me, you have no idea what this man is capable of."

"That's why we want to put him permanently out of commission," said Aubrey.

"I'm afraid I can't help you," said his father, standing up. "Now. I have a faculty meeting."

Aubrey took his coat off the tree and handed hers to Meredith. He shepherded her out the door.

"What is he afraid of?" asked Meredith in a hoarse whisper.

"Something huge. That wasn't like my father: Mr. Freedom of Information Act."

"What do we do now?" she asked.

"Well, as I see it, we only have two alternatives. The Serb community and the Mercantile Exchange. If he is in Chicago, and if he is alive, he must be known somewhere. What we need is a picture of the man."

"The Chicago Public Library has the *Tribune* on line," Meredith said. "Let's go back to the office and spend the rest of the afternoon researching Zoran Duric for ourselves. Maybe we'll come up with a photograph."

Aubrey and Meredith spent the afternoon going through digitized pages of the Chicago Tribune from the Bosnian War years. He took the year 1992, and she looked through 1993. It was like combing out a sheep dog—tedious and not easily rewarded. "He's mentioned," said Aubrey, strolling into Meredith's cubicle. "But there's no photo. Everything going on was so horrendous, he's just an 'also ran.'"

"Agreed. Same thing in '93. But we've got to keep going. I can't think of anything else to do. I'm only a quarter of the way through the year."

"You know," said Aubrey. "I can't help but think of my father's behavior. I think we convinced him that Duric is alive. He was pretty dismissive of the phone call and the White Paper. But you'd think he'd want the guy caught. I'm wondering if he has some kind of personal reason for not wanting us to hunt for him."

"You are his son," said Meredith. "He knows what a dangerous man Duric is. Maybe that's personal reason enough."

"What if he knows more than he's telling us? What if he's going to look for Duric himself?"

"How do you feel about that?"

"It worries me. A lot," said Aubrey.

"Do you have any reason to think he ran into Duric when he was a peacekeeper?"

Should I tell her my mother is a Serbian? That I suspect she knew him?

No. It's not my secret to tell.

"Not really. But he does seem sort of fixated on him, don't you think?" asked Aubrey.

"A bit. But I don't know him well. If you had been through what he's been through, wouldn't you feel an animus against all the war criminals? Especially one who probably faked his own death and got away with his crimes?"

"Yeah. I guess." He straightened up and found himself studying the hollow in Meredith's neck underneath her bun as she scrolled through the *Trib* on her computer.

She's so vulnerable. Something happened to her overseas. Something she won't talk about. How can I keep her safe if I don't know what memories she's fighting? If I don't know if Duric is alive?

At length, he went back to work. Finally, halfway through the year 1992, he found a fuzzy profile shot from a short distance captioned, "Bosnian-Serbian terrorist, Zoran Duric, rouses his countrymen to bloodshed."

His heart began to pound. From the grainy profile, he couldn't see much, but he could tell the man had a long, thin Roman nose and a high brow. Someone who knew him might recognize him in the picture, however. He printed it out and continued scanning the photos, hoping for another one.

Meredith came over to his workspace a few minutes later. "Find anything?" she asked.

"Just this." He handed her the printout.

Meredith squinted at the picture as though trying to get it in focus.

"He doesn't look familiar to me," she said.

Aubrey was doubtful. "How can you tell anything from that shot? It was obviously taken surreptitiously."

"Let's do a Google image search and see if we can get some more photos."

But by the end of the day, they had nothing more than the one blurry photo.

"This is useless," Aubrey said.

"You never know," Meredith told him. "I think we should canvass that Serbian neighborhood with it."

"We'll probably get a dozen hits at least," said Aubrey. "And they'll all be false leads."

"I still think we should try it," Meredith said.

"Okay, then. We'll go down there tomorrow."

"Okay. On another note, why don't I make us a stir fry tonight?" she asked. "I owe you for the use of your bed last night."

"Are you still afraid?" he asked, keeping his voice gentle.

"A little," she admitted.

"I think an evening of diversion is called for. Let's have a date. Do you by any chance like the symphony?"

"Yes! I love it!"

"I have tickets for Grieg's piano concerto tonight."

"You do? That would be great."

* * *

Orchestra Hall always set Aubrey's blood rushing with its early twentieth-century opulence. Sharing the experience with Meredith made him see and appreciate everything more—the grand chandelier, the gracefully arched ceiling, the plush red seats. It was all so civilized and a great diversion from war and genocide.

He helped Meredith off with her coat and checked it. Guiding her gently with his hand to the small of her back, he led her to their seats in the first balcony. She was gorgeous tonight, wearing a black dress that hugged her hips and flared at the knees. He didn't know much about women's fashion, but he thought she looked like a model.

"You should get out more," he said. "You look lovely."

He could see the blush spread across her cheeks. "Thank you. These are great seats. How did I not know you were a symphony aficionado?"

"Maybe you thought I was a philistine. But it's necessary to me. It soothes the beast," he said. "When things get horrible."

"What do you mean?"

"I have depressive tendencies. Music keeps my head in order."

She put a hand on his arm and turned in her seat to look into his face. Her blue-gray eyes were soft with compassion. "I had no idea."

"It's not something I advertise," he said, squirming inside. Why had he gone and admitted that? It was the whole reason he usually avoided relationships. He didn't want her pity.

"I'm sorry. I know how mean that beast can be. . ." The lights lowered. "Someday, I'll tell you," she whispered.

The Grieg with its thumping imperative soon captured his attention. Even so, he was aware of the woman at his side. He had kept his feelings for her in a tight container, never letting them out so he could examine them.

Now he noticed that when she thought he was fully absorbed by the concert, she took her little vial of hand sanitizer out of her clutch purse. She squeezed a tiny bit into her hands and spread it surreptitiously.

What was that all about? He knew full well she had OCD, but he couldn't remember that it had ever manifested during graduate school. Was it something that developed, or was one born with it?

The concerto came to a crashing end, and he leaped to his feet clapping and cheering, "Bravo!"

"That was sensational!" he said.

"I agree," she said with a smile. "What could possibly follow that?"

"We can leave now if you want. It's a couple of Hadyn symphonies after the interval."

"Let's," she said. "I didn't sleep much last night."

The old Illinois Athletic Club, now a charming hotel, had a great bar a few doors down from Orchestra Hall. It was a favorite haunt of his. They went inside its cozy fastness, and he ordered bourbon. As usual, Meredith had a cola.

"That was nice of you to invite me tonight. It was just what I needed."

"Me, too," he said. "Why is it you only drink cola?"

"Alcoholism runs in the family. I don't like to take chances."

"Oh. Sorry. I didn't mean to pry. It's your business, of course."

"People with depressive tendencies shouldn't drink, you know," she returned.

"I keep it to one a night," he said. "Don't fuss at me."

"Sorry. I just don't want to see you mess with that brilliant mind."

He made a face, and she said, "I'm serious."

"Let's talk about something else."

Her face immediately assumed its mask of worry, her brow furrowed, her generous mouth pinched. "How did Duric know I was trying to find him? How did he know my cell number?"

"You seem to be certain it was Duric who was calling."

"The voice mask sort of gave him away. I bought a new phone today. Taking a pen out of her clutch, she wrote the number on a napkin and gave it to him. He tucked it in his pocket. "Thanks."

"He could have gotten your number from the station," he said. "But how he found out you were looking for him, I have no idea."

* * *

When they returned to her condo, she picked up her mail which she had neglected to do earlier.

"Open that," he said, indicating the uppermost envelope addressed by hand in block capitals.

Her brow lowered as she stared at it. Then using her thumb, she broke the seal and opened the letter.

A photo of her, used by the *Tribune* when she won broadcasting award, fell out of the envelope. A red line slashed across her image.

"Fingerprints," he said. "Hold it by the corners and stick it in the envelope again. That may have DNA on the sticky stuff."

Throwing down the mail, she raced up the stairs, negotiated the three locks on her door, and he saw her race to the bathroom. Sounds of vomiting reached him.

CHAPTER SIX

After spending half an hour in the bathroom, scrubbing everything thoroughly and doing her breathing exercises, she was finally ready to face her guest.

"So much for our soothing evening," she said, trying to keep her voice steady.

Aubrey's face was a thundercloud. "We're going to the police this time. Tonight, if you like."

"I think tomorrow will be soon enough." Meredith strove to be reasonable. "He's stalking me if he knows where I live."

"Tonight, I'm on *your* couch," he said.

She turned on all the lights and looked through her condo. As far as she could tell, nothing had been touched.

"Tomorrow you're taking me to buy a gun."

"All right," he said, resignation burdening his voice.

Meredith went to the linen closet outside her bedroom and took out a set of sheets. Without saying anything further, she pulled out the hide-a-bed and made it up. For warmth, she added two of her mother's quilts.

She crossed her arms over her chest and hugged herself against a sudden shiver. "You should be comfortable here. I appreciate your staying."

"Don't be uneasy," said Aubrey. "I'm no predator."

"I know you aren't. This whole situation just reminds me how vulnerable I am. When I was in the Mideast, I learned to keep my guard up at all times. I hate living this way."

Saying nothing, Aubrey went to the kitchen, pulled the milk out of the refrigerator, found a latte cup in the cupboard and proceeded to make his mother's soothing drink for her again. Even through all her layers of anxiety, she was touched by his kindness.

But she couldn't allow herself to feel anything more. Never again. She must concentrate on Zoran Duric. Her plate was full. She was not in any way ready for romance. Even with the appealing Aubrey.

"We're going to drag this guy out into the light," she said to him. Even she could feel the hardness in her voice. "I'm not going to be intimidated."

"Atta girl!" he said. "But I have the feeling you're fighting Goliaths inside while you're trying with all your might to keep the lid on."

She bit her lip and turned her head away. "I'm not ready to talk about it, Aubrey. Maybe someday."

"Does it have anything to do with your OCD? I don't remember your having it before you went overseas."

She forced a little laugh. That she could talk about. "I got e. Coli and h pylori in Africa at the refugee camp. I was pretty sick. I had an ulcer and lost a lot of weight. I'm pretty careful about keeping random bacteria out of my life now. I know I'm a bit extreme."

"Ugh. I don't blame you for being careful. I'm surprised you didn't come home after that."

"No. The Red Cross had the antibiotics I needed. They were almost worse than the diseases."

He put his head to one side and looked at her searchingly. She kept "the lid on it," though and didn't tell him what he wanted to know.

"So," she said. "We go down to the South Side tomorrow?"

"Yeah. But it's probably a fool's errand."

Putting his hands on her shoulders, he drew her to him and kissed her cheek. His hands and his lips, though gentle, burned like a brand on her skin. He looked into her eyes. She didn't know what he read there, but she felt it necessary to say, "I'm not looking for romance, Aubrey."

He gave her a rueful smile. "Neither am I, but it seems I can't help myself."

She took his hands off her shoulders and squeezed them. "Try," she said. "Or it will make things really awkward."

"It would help if you just told me to get lost."

She blinked back sudden tears. "But I don't want you to," she said softly. She walked out of the room and into the kitchen where she grabbed the butcher knife. Then, Aubrey watching, she went to her bedroom and closed the door.

Ghosts visited her, and it was a long time before she fell asleep, kitchen knife under her pillow.

* * *

When she woke up, Aubrey had made German pancakes with powdered sugar for breakfast along with a side of scrambled eggs.

"Oh, yum," said Meredith. "You're trying to fatten me up."

"Guilty," he said. "I called in to Mary Ann and left a message for Mr. Q about what we're doing today. But first, we're going to the police with that envelope."

"Right," she said, shuddering.

* * *

Police Officer Kearns, a red-headed Irishman at Chicago police headquarters listened to their story.

"This sounds like a case for the FBI," he said.

"We went to them yesterday. Before the envelope came," said Aubrey. He took Agent Werner's card out of his wallet and handed it to Officer Kearns. "Basically, they told us it's not a priority, but they will be there for the takedown if we call them."

Kearns swore. "Officious idiots," he added. "I'm going to give this guy a call. You can wait in the break room if you want to. There's coffee, but I can't vouch for it."

Meredith and Aubrey went to the room indicated and sat.

"I don't think I'll touch the coffee," he said.

"Me neither," she agreed. "He was pretty ticked off. I'm glad he took it seriously."

"I'm sure he wants to use the FBI's database—IAFIS and their DNA records."

"IAFIS?" she asked.

"Fingerprints of anyone who was ever booked worked for the government or was in the military."

"I'm not hopeful about that," said Meredith. "Or the DNA. They won't have a sample to match with."

"You're probably right," said Aubrey.

Officer Kearns came back to the break room.

"Werner says to messenger the envelope to him, so I'll do that and wait to hear from him. I don't suppose I can convince you to sit at home behind a locked door, Ms. Montgomery?"

"I have a job," she said.

The officer gave Aubrey back the agent's card and gave them both one of his own.

"Use some sense and let us know what you find."

Aubrey pulled back his jacket to show the officer his empty holster. "I checked my Glock at the door," he said.

"You have a conceal carry license; I take it?"

"Sure do," said Aubrey. "And I don't intend to let her out of my sight."

"I would like to buy a gun myself," said Meredith. "I think, under the circumstances that it may come in handy."

"You can't take possession of it until 72 hours after purchase here in Illinois. And you will need to fill out a Firearms Owners Identification Card. It won't take long. Come back to my desk."

Half an hour later, they were thanking Officer Kearns and leaving the Precinct.

* * *

"Where do we go from here?" asked Meredith as they left the police station.

"We're going southeast on the expressway to a town called Lansing. It used to have a huge Serbian community, and they built one of the first Serbian Orthodox Churches. I thought if we could meet with the priest there, he might guide us to benevolent societies that might be able to help us get 'the word on the street' about Duric."

"That sounds like a good plan," she said. "I didn't sleep well last night. Do you mind if I put on my earbuds and listen to some Bach? It helps relax me."

"Plug your phone into my speaker system. I love Bach for the same reason. He evens out my crazies. There is something elemental and predictable about him."

He helped her do as he asked and soon the sounds of a chamber orchestra surrounded them. She put her head back on the seat and let the music soothe her "crazies." She had never had a name for them before.

In the light Saturday traffic, it didn't take long to reach Lansing, and the Serbian Orthodox Church was its defining feature. White plastered with two hexagonal towers, it had the air of a "mother" church, sitting on a large tract of lawn.

They parked and walked inside. Meredith caught her breath. The interior of the church was stunning. With a midnight blue background, the domed ceiling was painted with closely-placed icons of Mary and other saints trimmed in gold leaf.

A man in a floor-length black robe approached them, his long white beard and black headdress identifying him as an Orthodox priest. To Meredith, the sight of him in this setting took her away to Serbia when she had visited Belgrade one summer during her undergraduate years.

"Greetings," the priest said, his voice heavy with its Slavic accent. "May I help you?"

Meredith realized she had given no thought to what she would say. She jerked herself into the present moment as Aubrey was saying, "Good morning, Father. I am Aubrey Kettering, and this is Ms. Meredith Montgomery. We are journalists from WOOT TV doing a story on the evolution of the Chicago communities that made up the former

Yugoslavia. Could you direct us to the head of the Serb National Federation or the Serbian Sisters of St. Archangel Michael?"

"I, myself, am an expert on that subject."

Meredith asked, "Would you be willing to talk to us, then?"

"I have an hour before I celebrate the twelve o'clock service. Would you care to come with me to my office?"

They followed him down the nave of the church out a little door behind the altarpiece. Meredith found herself in a small, but comfortable room in midnight blue, lit by one small, high window and several electric candles. She and Aubrey sat on a gold velvet loveseat, while the priest seated himself behind a heavy Victorian-style desk. The smell of incense had penetrated here from the sanctuary.

"I understand that many of the Serbs have integrated into towns around the area like South Holland and Palos Hills," said Aubrey. Meredith, still shaken from last night's threat and her sleepless night, admired Aubrey's research and preparation for this interview.

"Yes. It has taken over a century, but my countrymen are becoming fully integrated into Chicago's society. Some of them even live on the North Shore."

The priest proceeded to relate a short history of the Serbs in Chicago. First, they had come from the old country to work in the steel mills. Gradually, they had become an educated people and became upwardly mobile. Lansing itself was a step up from their initial settlements in West Town, Joliet, and Gary. Until Tito died, they had still retained a Slavic sense of community. Then Yugoslavia began to sliver, and the "fratricide" had begun among the all the different ethnicities that had made up their country since President Wilson had created it after World War I at the fall of the Austro-Hungarian Empire.

"That was very bad for my country. The world judged Serbians to be barbarians, when, in fact, except for a handful of madmen, we are a profoundly religious people."

"I understand there are far fewer people who wish to be identified as Serbian these days," said Aubrey.

"That is true. Many have moved to other cities. Our Serbian population in Chicago has reduced greatly. The ones who are still here have assimilated into the population. I shepherd a very devout congregation, but they are mostly elderly. I don't know what will happen to this beautiful church when they begin to die off."

"Did many Serbs come here from Bosnia after the war?"

"A few. They are middle-aged now, like me. That is when I came."

Meredith exchanged glances with Aubrey. He gave a slight nod. She opened her briefcase and removed a copy of the picture from the *Tribune* of Zoran Duric. Standing, she laid it on the priest's desk. "Have you ever seen this man?"

The priest took out small wire-rimmed reading glasses and perched them on his nose. He turned on a banker's lamp on his desk and held the picture under its green shade.

The priest looked up slowly. "This is a very bad, very dangerous man. What is your business with him?"

"I received an anonymous call from someone who saw him on Michigan Avenue, said Meredith. "He said he was guilty of genocide. The caller identified himself as a Bosnian Serb."

"He is in the U.S., this man?" He pointed to the picture. "Where did this come from?"

"It was in the *Chicago Tribune.* An Associated Press photograph taken in 1992 in Bosnia. It was the only picture I could find of the man the caller identified as Zoran Duric."

"You are searching for him. That is why you have come."

Meredith swallowed. "Yes. We didn't think he'd be part of your community, but we thought maybe someone might have seen him."

"Ah, this one would not associate with the people here. He grew very, very rich in the war. He looted churches and museums. He took everything of any value for himself and his men. He was one of that handful of bad Serbs I told you of. If he is living in the U.S., it is among the wealthy."

"We have heard conflicting reports," Aubrey said. "Some say Muslims killed him in Sarajevo after the war."

"He went to Belgrade after the war. That is when I knew him. He was very rich, and also very unhappy with the Dayton Peace. Then he disappeared. Some say he went to Switzerland with all his gold. But it is possible that he has come here and goes by another identity."

"And you don't think he would have been in touch with any of the Serbs in this community?" asked Aubrey.

"It would be better if I asked the questions of my people. Do you have another copy of this picture?"

Meredith assured him that they did. "That would be very helpful if you could do that. We are afraid that he may be planning something in this country. Possibly against the Muslims."

"That would not surprise me at all. The Muslims have been much in the news, and he has a burning, irrational hatred of them. He feels they won the Bosnian War."

"He has threatened Ms. Montgomery's life," said Aubrey. "So we would really appreciate it if you would ask your questions sooner than later."

The priest promised that he would, and with many thanks for his help, Aubrey and Meredith made their way out of the remarkable church.

"That was a stroke of luck, running into him," said Aubrey.

"Yes. It shortened our work by a lot," said Meredith. "Now we have time to buy my gun."

"Anything to make you feel more secure. Best thing to do is find a sporting goods store in the suburbs."

The rest of the afternoon was taken up with buying Meredith her own Glock and arranging to take delivery of it in three days.

Aubrey congratulated her. "I can't wait to see you shoot."

"I got to be pretty handy with a Beretta overseas, but this Glock is a whole lot heftier. I think it will take some getting used to."

"Let's grab dinner at O'Henry's, and we can discuss our next move," said Aubrey.

"Good idea. How long before I can get a conceal carry permit?"

"You have to take a class. It's not a short little thing, either. Sixteen hours."

* * *

To Meredith's delight, they sighted Allie at their booth under the Prohibition poster. She went over and made her friend stand up for a hug.

Aubrey ordered a beer and Meredith a cola. It occurred to her that it was unusual to see Allie out alone. She was nearly always accompanied by the boyfriend of the moment.

"What are you doing in here, drinking alone?" asked Meredith.

"Stood up," she said briefly. Obviously, she didn't want to discuss it because she said, "You still on the tail of that Serbian guy?"

"Yeah," Meredith answered. "We went down to one of the old Serbian neighborhoods today and met a priest who's going to help us out. This is one bad guy, Allie. Even the Serbs think he's bad. The priest knew him, but he's never seen him in Chicago. He's going to ask around for us."

"Her life was threatened last night," Aubrey said. "She actually bought a gun today."

"Whoa. You think it was this guy? Zoran whatever?"

"Duric," said Meredith. She told her friend what had been in the mail last night. "Yeah, I don't know who else would be threatening my life. The mystery is that he knew where to find me. And he's been calling me, too."

"You're being stalked!" Allie said, her face alive with outrage. "No wonder you got a gun! Tell me about this guy. What have you found out?"

Aubrey related the facts they had gathered from their sources, including the priest.

"Shouldn't the FBI be taking care of this?"

"They don't consider it a priority," said Meredith. "They have enough Chicago crime to keep them busy. They can't be bothered with a random Serb who committed genocide."

"I don't blame you for being bitter," said Allie. "Especially after you've been threatened."

Aubrey broke in, "I think we should question the Bosnian Muslims next. The internet says they have a mosque in Northbrook. That could be a target."

"That makes sense in a crazy kind of way," said Allie. "This whole thing is nuts. I wonder if that anonymous caller knew what he was getting you into."

Aubrey got a thoughtful look in his eye and tilted his head to one side. "That's a really good question. Maybe he knew something was up with this dude."

"Maybe he's Muslim and not a Serb!" said Meredith.

"We're getting carried away, here," said Aubrey. "Let's eat."

They all ordered corn beef with cabbage and fries.

"How have you been feeling lately?" Allie asked Meredith. "I know h pylori is the devil to get rid of."

"I haven't been tested lately. But it doesn't feel like I have my ulcer anymore."

"Good."

Meredith wished her friend wouldn't look at her so searchingly. She knew Allie wanted to ask about the state of her broken heart, but fortunately, she didn't.

"Program for tomorrow," said Aubrey. "A: We check with police to see if they got anything off the letter. B: We go to visit the Muslim mosque in Northbrook."

"Sounds good to me," said Meredith.

CHAPTER SEVEN

Aubrey insisted that he spend the night on Meredith's hide-a-bed again.

"I have to admit," she said, "I feel a lot safer with you here. I don't think I'd be able to fall asleep otherwise."

Aubrey had made a decision. "There is something I think I must tell you, in the interests of complete honesty," he said as he helped her pull out the bed.

"You like hide-a-beds, and you would rather sleep on one than your expensive mattress."

He laughed. He realized he hadn't laughed all day. He didn't want to introduce a somber note, but he felt the time had come that he take her into his family's confidence.

"Let's sit down on the couch-couch. And could you turn on the gas fire in the fireplace?"

"It's cold, isn't it?" She knelt by the fireplace and, after turning on the gas, lit the fire with a long match, especially for the purpose. Then she came and sat by him.

"You have probably wondered, especially after our visit with the priest today, why I know so much about the Serbs."

"I was wondering when you had the time to do all that research. We've been practically living in each other's pockets."

"My mother is a Serb," he said. "Though she prefers that no one know. I even speak Serbo-Croatian."

Meredith took in this information. "Did your father meet her when he was with the U.N. peacekeeping force?"

"Yes. After the war. Her parents had been 'ethnically cleansed' during the siege in Sarajevo."

Meredith's brow was lowered as she looked at him, her blue-gray eyes soft with compassion. "How horrible that must have been for her!"

"It was. I am certain she was assaulted. But she had a stroke of luck when she met my father, and he fell in love with her. He married her there. I was actually born there. Then Dad brought her back to the States with him. But for the last twenty-five years, she has been plagued with horrible nightmares. She has been in and out of the psych ward, but nothing helps to get rid of them."

"PTSD," said Meredith.

"Yes. And there's more. My father knows Zoran Duric, I'm certain of it. Not only does he want us to leave him alone, he told me not to mention him to my mother."

"Oh. My. Gosh. That's terrible. She must have known him!" she said. "Does your dad really mind that we're working on it?"

"I have a history of not taking his advice. I have inherited a lot of things from my mother, and stubbornness is one of them."

"The depression?" she asked.

"That, too. It kind of goes with the Slavic makeup."

"Rachmaninoff, Tchaikovsky, and Shostakovich," she said. "It's in all of their music. Is there anything you can do about the depression?"

"There are medications. My mother has been on and off many since the war. She finally seems to be stable, so I am taking the same cocktail of meds she is on. They are helping. A lot. I don't want you to be worried about her or about me."

"That's why you don't want to be in a relationship, isn't it?" she asked.

"Yes," Aubrey admitted, feeling a whoosh of relief at having the facts out in the open. "I don't want to pass it on to my children."

"But it needn't be a handicap, now that you know which meds work for you."

His spirits lifted. "You really think that?"

Her whole face was lit from within. "Yes. And so should you. They are finding better and better meds all the time. Depression is an illness. I have to take meds, too, for my OCD."

"And we've seen how well those work," he teased.

"Well, you should see me without them! I can't even think of eating in a restaurant or working in an office with other people."

"The refugee camps were really bad, then?"

"Nothing like what you see on TV. Much worse. And, for the most part, hopeless. In Africa, at least."

"It was better in the Middle East?" he asked, surprised.

Her face underwent a change. It was like a curtain was pulled over it. "I . . . I don't . . . can't talk about that."

So *there* was the problem. Something had happened there. She sat stiff and straight as a rod. Her eyes were full of misery.

"Message received," he said. "Private territory. No trespassing."

"I'm sorry. You've been so open with me and I appreciate it far more than I can say. But I'm not ready to share. I haven't even told my mom everything. We were both swallowed up in grief over my father's death at the same time."

"We are a sad pair," he said, suddenly deflated.

"But we are doing something useful. We are hunting down a man with no conscience, a man with a huge capacity for evil." There was no mistaking her earnest intent. "You know the saying, 'All that it takes for evil to prevail is for good men to do nothing.'"

He smiled at her. "But there's more to life than duty, though you might not feel it now. There's joy, too."

Aubrey wanted very much to kiss her, but he managed to restrain himself. She had told him she wasn't ready. He just had to hope that some time she *would* be ready, because he wanted it more than anything he could think of, at the moment.

Changing the subject, he said, "You mentioned at the outset that there might be a trip to Sarajevo in all of this. Why?"

"We will need specific charges against this man if he is to be put on trial for war crimes. That means witness interviews," Meredith said, her voice weary. "And, of course, we need them for our story."

"That won't be any fun. Though I am interested in seeing how Bosnia has fared under reconstruction in the last twenty-five years. I could also visit the place I was born."

"I thought you were born in Sarajevo."

He ran a hand through his hair. "Actually, I was born in a village outside the capital. Sarajevo was a ruin, and my mother was living in a shell of their house with no plumbing or electricity. When my parents were married, my father moved her to Votopad, outside the city. He managed to find something for them that was habitable. I can't even imagine what would have happened to my mother if she hadn't met and married my father."

"It sounds grim, that's for sure," said Meredith, chin on hands, elbows on knees.

He was drawing tiny circles on her back with his fingers when his phone rang. Checking caller ID, he saw with surprise that it was his mother. Her ears must have been burning.

"Hello, Mom."

"Darling, I'm sorry to interrupt your Saturday evening, but I had to speak to you. My friend, Malena, just phoned me and asked if I knew you had been questioning Father Savic about Zoran Duric today! He is a monster! Father Savic asked Malena if she knew where Duric was living in Chicago. You must stop this at once!"

Aubrey's heart raced as though he had been caught doing something naughty.

"Mom, I have an explanation. It's work. My partner and I can come tomorrow after your church, and I will explain it to you. Do you go to Father Savic's church down in Lansing?"

"I do. It has always been a great comfort to me."

"I'm glad. I liked him. What time will you be home?"

"I will go to ten o'clock service so that I can be home by noon. I will make a pot roast in my slow cooker. You may bring your excellent bread pudding with raspberry sauce."

"Okay, Mom. We'll see you tomorrow. Try not to worry."

He ended the call before she could expostulate that of course, she would worry.

Turning to Meredith, he said, "I should have figured out that would have happened eventually. Mom heard from a friend about our inquiries with the priest today. I have been commanded to bring you to dinner tomorrow at noon and to bring my bread pudding with raspberry sauce. She aims to talk me out of this."

"Your father must be furious," she said.

"I imagine he is," Aubrey said with a sigh. He inevitably displeased his father, ever since he had left the South Side for j-school at Northwestern.

"Bread pudding has to sit overnight, doesn't it?"

"Yes. It doesn't require much by way of ingredients—do you have bread, sugar, and eggs? Oh, and nutmeg. I can make the raspberry sauce tomorrow."

She stood. "What a nice interruption of our morbid thoughts. Yes, I have all those things. Lead on, Chef."

* * *

If Meredith had a stalker, Aubrey didn't want to take the chance of leading him to his family home and his mother. Aubrey drove Meredith and the bread pudding in his well-muscled Mustang to David's house and exchanged it for Paula's Silver Honda Accord. He had promised Paula he would start it up every few days while she and David were on their honeymoon so the battery wouldn't die.

With two hours to kill, they decided to take a nice drive up Sheridan Road. A black Tahoe stayed behind them a few cars back, but it could be a family out for a Sunday drive.

Not until they turned west at Lake Forest did the car separate itself from the pack to follow them. Aubrey had skills. He had played "Ditch 'Em" with his friends growing up where they practiced outwitting each other in Chicago traffic. As he drove through the western suburbs, he managed to elude his tail before jumping on the expressway and weaving between the lanes until they reached downtown. From that point, he took Lake Shore Drive down to his parents' home. He had lost the black Tahoe.

He wondered what Meredith thought of his home. It was in Hyde Park—a three-story, sky blue clapboard. By Hyde Park standards, it was a mansion, with its own park-type garden.

His mother met them at the door, looking striking in a black floor-length skirt and blouse. When she saw Meredith, her cheeks flushed with pleasure. She extended her hand and introduced herself, "I'm Stana Kettering; you must call me Stana."

Meredith shook her hand and said, "I'm Aubrey's work colleague, Meredith Montgomery."

Aubrey's dad stood at his mother's elbow, and it was Meredith's turn to blush. "Dr. Kettering! I didn't tell you this when we met in your office, but I feel as though I know you professionally. I studied the Balkans as an undergraduate. We used your book and your essays. I have even heard you speak."

"Meredith," he nodded and shook her hand. "It's good to see you again. Come in, come in. We have Stana's wonderful pot roast, and I see that you have brought the bread pudding, Aubrey. Outstanding."

Aubrey watched as Meredith took in the lovely surroundings of his home. The floors were hardwood with only area rugs, European style. The furniture was modern leather and chrome. The art on the walls was abstract and notable for its bold colors.

"What a lovely home you have," she said. "And that pot roast smells heavenly."

The dining room table was set with china, silver, and crystal. Evidently, his mother considered the occasion a formal one. They sat down to dinner immediately, and his mother asked him to bless the food, which he did perfunctorily. Meredith looked at him in amusement.

By unspoken agreement, they did not discuss the business of Zoran Duric at the table. Instead, his father asked him questions about his research for the TV station, and Aubrey asked his father about his research for a paper he was to present next summer in Copenhagen.

His mother didn't talk and ate little which worried Aubrey. She kept stealing glances at Meredith, and he wondered if his guest noticed. Meredith was dressed nicely in a casual oatmeal-colored turtleneck sweater and black slacks. She wore a gold bangle on her wrist and a necklace made of complicated gold chain.

After the bread pudding, which his mother pronounced excellent, they adjourned to what he had always thought of as the family room. There was a fire going in the marble fireplace, and his mother's cello sat out.

"Play something for us, Mom?" he asked.

She nodded and sat at the cello. Placing the bow on the strings, she played something Slavic that flowed through the room with melancholy. They all clapped.

His dad said, "When Stana came from Bosnia, she didn't come empty-handed. She had her marvelous talent."

His mom beamed. Then her face turned serious, and she said, "We must talk about Bosnia, though I try to avoid it when I can."

"Tell us about this man, Mom. Tell us what you know."

She took a deep breath. "Zoran Duric is my brother. Your uncle."

Aubrey inhaled sharply, and he felt Meredith start beside him.

"I wish with all my heart it were not so, but I am afraid it is. Father Savic says he has been seen in Chicago."

"Yes," Aubrey said. "At least we think so. An anonymous caller informed Meredith of the fact."

He prodded Meredith who told them the story so far, including their visits to the police and the FBI. Aubrey told them about the defaced newspaper portrait Meredith had received in the mail.

"This is a very grave matter," said his father. "Duric kills without compunction. He has no conscience. He is the worst kind of criminal. You can see why we have cut all ties with him. He is playing a game with you, trying to increase your terror, Meredith."

"I believe you," she said. "I *am* terrified. Aubrey took me to buy a gun yesterday."

Stana put her hands to her face and shook with sudden sobs. "You must get away. Let the FBI catch him."

"As a matter of fact," said Aubrey, "We are going to Sarajevo. We need to collect evidence of his crimes to convince the FBI that he is a serious criminal. Has he done anything since the war?"

"Oh, yes. I am sure he continues to terrorize the Muslims. He hates them. They killed our parents and brutalized me, and that started it, but he developed an overwhelming obsession for hurting them. If he is here, it has something to do with the Muslims. There are so many refugees coming here just now."

"We thought perhaps he lived here under an assumed name," said Meredith.

"He may," said Stana. "He went to Belgrade when the peace was signed. He had stolen much gold and many antiquities from the churches and museums. He was rich.

He could have lived anywhere. He had a child. Perhaps he wanted to bring it up in America."

"Hmm," said Aubrey. "That's interesting. A child. What happened to its mother?"

"I never knew. I don't even know what gender or age the child is."

"Before we leave for Sarajevo, we will find some way to warn the Bosnian Muslim community," Aubrey promised. "What else can you tell us about your brother? Can you give us any ideas about who we should interview in Bosnia?"

She said, "Mr. Ibram Ibrisimovic is a prominent Bosniak in Sarajevo. He would know who you should talk to."

Aubrey tapped the name into his phone.

"That is a tremendous help, Stana," said Meredith. "You are very brave. Do you think your brother has any idea you are here?"

"I don't know," she answered. "You must know this Aubrey. We changed our name. It used to be Wilson. I have been hiding from him ever since I left Sarajevo. Somehow, I think he must have found out I am in Chicago. It is his way to terrorize people. I am certain that is what he is doing to Meredith."

"Well, it's working," said Meredith.

Aubrey asked, "When was the last time you saw him? What happened?"

Stana was rubbing her hands up and down her arms as though she were cold. With the fire, it was quite warm. "I haven't seen him since your father married me and moved me to Votopad. Even though I hated what the Muslims did to me, I wanted him caught for the horrible atrocities he was committing. I no longer considered him family. He must have found out I was cooperating with the U.N. If he ever finds out who we are, he will kill us, Aubrey. Our whole family." Tears smudged her careful makeup as they fell unchecked.

Meredith turned to Aubrey. "I think we should leave for Sarajevo as soon as we can manage. But we must go there indirectly. We don't want him to know where we're going."

"Good idea. We can book tickets to Paris and go from there," Aubrey said, liking the idea.

"Good," said his father. "I still don't like this, but at this point, you don't have any choice but going after him. He is not going to stop terrorizing you. And once he sees you, he will guess who you are, Aubrey. You have your mother's eyes and the same shape to your face."

"The Muslims in Sarajevo may even know where he is in Chicago. They may have eyes on him," said Stana.

"That would be a bonus," said Meredith. "Even if we gather enough evidence against him, we still need to know where he is."

The idea of Meredith being terrorized chilled Aubrey to the bone. "I'll go make some reservations to Paris," said Aubrey. "We'll go see the Imam at the Islamic Cultural Center in Northbrook tomorrow morning. Then we'll fly. We'll stay in France a day or two, then go to Sarajevo from there."

"Perfect," said his mother. "When will you leave?"

"I think the sooner, the better, under the circumstances. Tomorrow, if I can get a flight," Aubrey said.

"That sounds prudent," said his father. "You may borrow my den to make your reservations right now. I am glad you are being so proactive about this."

CHAPTER EIGHT

With Aubrey watching from Paula's Honda, Meredith walked up the steps to her home Sunday evening. She tried to shake off the feeling that she was being watched. She ran up the stairs, unlocked her three locks, and entered her condo. Throwing the deadbolt fast, she leaned against the door, taking a deep, shaky breath. The blinds were all down, so she didn't hesitate to flip the switches beside her, flooding the rooms with light.

He's out there. I know he's out there.

Once she had changed into jeans and a Fair Isle sweater, she tried to eat some crackers and brie, while watching the shaded windows for shadows.

Her phone rang in the pocket of her jeans. With dread, she drew it out and looked at the number. It was blocked. After a moment she answered.

She heard the Darth Vader-like breathing again. She knew it was only the sound of a voice-altering filter, and the man said nothing this time. After fifteen seconds of her unanswered "hellos", the caller hung up.

Trembling and clammy, she wished Aubrey were with her. She couldn't eat. Taking her dishes to the sink, Meredith rinsed the items for the dishwasher.

After a moment of scanning her kitchen, she grabbed her butcher knife, walked upstairs, and went into the bathroom and locked the door. Sitting on the closed toilet, she gripped her hands together.

Meredith had worked on exposés before, but never one that was as potentially explosive as this one. She was on the verge of uncovering things long buried.

If you can't stand the heat, get out of the kitchen. Investigative journalism isn't for wimps.

While she was getting ready to take a bath, her phone was rang in the pocket of her pants. By the time she got to it, the caller had hung up. Checking the number, she realized it was Aubrey.

Great. The one person I want *to call me.*

She called him back.

"Sorry," she said when he answered. "I couldn't get to the phone."

"That's all right. Just wanted to know if you were okay."

The tub needed a good scrubbing. She turned on the water. "I'm not, actually. We need to get out of town. I know he was out there when I got home tonight."

"Do you want me to come over?"

She wanted it more than anything.

Meredith tried to sound businesslike. "I'm trying to keep busy. I'll be fine. The door's locked."

"You going to scrub the tub?" he asked.

"How did you know?"

"I could hear it draining in the background, and I'm well acquainted with your OCD."

"Now you've made my night. Remind me not to phone you back next time." She disconnected the call. She had no defenses left against this man. And she was going to be traveling to the deepest, darkest Balkans with him. Was she nuts?

She got out the cleanser and tackled the tub.

* * *

Meredith was too keyed up to sleep. At two a.m., she gave up and went to her computer where she downloaded maps and travel guides to Paris and Bosnia onto her tablet, stopped her mail, and e-mailed her friend in the next condo, asking her to keep an eye on her place. Finally, she was tired enough to sleep. There was plenty of time tomorrow to pack.

CHAPTER NINE

Meredith was late to work, and Aubrey was worried. Finally, he gave up and called her. When she answered he was surprised that she sounded as though she had been asleep.

"Did I wake you? Are you feeling all right?" he asked.

"Oh my gosh! I went to bed about four and I didn't set my alarm! Give me an hour and I'll see you at the station."

"Have you packed yet?"

"No. Wow. I'm really messed up today."

"Never mind. I'll go talk to Mr. Q about the trip myself. You needed that sleep. Especially because we'll be traveling all night tonight. Get your packing done and I'll pick you up about three. We'll go visit the Islamic Center, and then have an early dinner before we go to O'Hare."

"Okay. Sorry to bail on you this morning."

"It's not a problem."

When their boss was brought up to date on the investigation and the threats against Meredith, he said, "I'd say you definitely need to get off this guy's radar. Especially with your mother involved. Your plan sounds good. This has the makings of a decent story. Especially, if you find a threat to the Muslims here in Chicago."

He took the train home and packed. He wished he could take his Glock, but there was no way with the restrictions on weapons when flying internationally.

He took an Uber to Meredith's condo and found her ready to go.

"I'm starting to look forward to Paris," she said.

He was glad to see that she looked rested for the first time in days. He should have ignored her and come over last night. He was sure she had been more spooked than she let on.

He kissed her cheek. "Let's go then."

His Uber was waiting for them. They drove to the suburb of Northbrook where the Cultural Center was located. Aubrey was surprised by its large size and very modern architecture. Constructed of red brick with lovely arches, it even had a minaret.

When they walked inside the glass doors, they found a modestly dressed woman in a black hijab and dress sitting at the receptionist's desk.

He said, "We are concerned citizens who have information about a possible threat to the Center." He pulled out his photo of Zoran Duric.

"This is a very old photo taken from the newspaper twenty-five years ago. I imagine the subject has far less hair, but have you seen anyone resembling him hanging about? His name is Zoran Duric. He's a Bosnian Serb with a horrific grudge."

The woman's beautiful brown eyes enlarged, and she took the newspaper photo.

"No. It is hard to tell, though."

Aubrey passed over his card and Meredith's. "Could we see the Imam? As you can see, we're TV reporters, but we are here in a private capacity."

She nodded and took up her telephone. Pressing a button, she spoke into the phone in Serbo-Croatian. Aubrey was very glad he understood what she said. She warned the Imam that they were reporters and said that their reason for seeing him seemed to be manufactured so that he should be on his guard. She recommended that he send Khalid out to check them for weapons before showing him into the Imam's presence.

A very large man he presumed to be Khalid came out of a door to the right of the receptionist a few moments later.

His English was heavily accented as he said, "Do you carry any weapons? I am the Imam's bodyguard, you understand."

"No," Aubrey said. "We are unarmed."

"You will please remove your coats?"

They took off the light trench coats they wore and handed them over. Khalid's eyes raked their forms, looking for concealed weapons as he checked all their coat pockets. He handed their outerwear back to them and said, "You will please to follow me."

Leading them through a wood-paneled corridor, he took them back to a comfortable office furnished with leather couches and a simple teak coffee table.

"The Imam will be with you in a moment," Khalid said, seating himself in a chair by the door.

Soon, a small man with a white taqiya on his head and a black robe appeared in the office. Aubrey and Meredith rose.

He nodded and sat across from them. They seated themselves.

"I am Imam."

"We are here to warn you," said Aubrey.

"Warn me?"

"You and your congregation," Aubrey said. "May I ask how recently you have come from Bosnia?"

He raised heavy black brows. "How do you know I come from Bosnia?"

"I speak Serbo-Croatian. My mother taught me. You have her accent."

"Ah. I have been in this country for twenty years."

Meredith spoke, "You were in Bosnia during the war, then?"

"Yes. In the siege of Sarajevo."

Aubrey nodded. "Did you ever hear of a man called Zoran Duric?"

The Imam bowed his head and put up a hand to shield his eyes. He didn't speak but drew a long breath. When he took away his hand, there were tears running down his face. Taking a handkerchief out of his pocket, he dabbed at his cheeks.

"Yes. I have heard of him."

"Then you will know what a dangerous man he is. I am sorry to tell you he is presently in Chicago. He is terrorizing my colleague, Ms. Montgomery, but we think his ultimate purpose is to do harm, possibly to your beautiful cultural center. If you know of him, you know that he enjoys hurting Bosniaks."

"The man is a terrorist," said the Imam.

"He is. We are leaving the country today, but we wanted to put you on your guard. You may want to call the police to have them patrol by the Center during the night until he is caught. Officer Kearns with the Chicago police is aware of this man's presence in the city."

"I will take your advice." The man rose. "Thank you for coming to warn me."

As he left the room, Aubrey had a feeling that the Imam had barely been holding on to his persona as a man of peace. He was visibly frightened.

Their duty done, they called another Uber to take them to O'Henry's for an early dinner.

He wished they could leave Zoran Duric and all his hatred out of their life and carry on as before, but he knew now that his own family was in danger. If he hadn't taken evasive maneuvers yesterday, he and Meredith could have led the stalker straight to his family.

"Has anyone been following us?" asked Meredith. "I was afraid to look."

"I don't think so. But if they have, we'll lose them at the airport. They have to have a boarding pass to get past security."

"So what did you think of the Imam?" he asked.

"He had a very difficult time with his emotions. I am guessing he knows Duric in a personal way."

"You're right, I think. I sure hope he can protect that Center. It must have cost the earth to build," he said.

"It is very impressive. Quite an achievement."

"Quite a target," said Aubrey. "Almost irresistible."

"I hope your mom is going to be safe, Aubrey. If Duric has seen you and learned your name, it will be child's play to find her."

He felt his brow gather. "I'm worried. I wish my father would take her away somewhere."

"He seems very protective of her. Maybe he will."

"One thing about my father is that he moves as slow as molasses in January. He weighs everything. He is ponderous. I hope he won't wait too long."

* * *

They arrived at O'Hare in plenty of time for the complicated security measures involved in international travel. International flight security was slow, and by the time they reached their gate in a distant terminal it was almost time to board.

After they were aboard, Meredith said, "I hope you don't mind, but I have an airplane play list and noise-cancelling headphones. It's the only way I can cope with being so many thousands of feet into the air."

"What's on your playlist?"

"Just some New Age relaxation stuff. Spa music," she said.

"Have at it. I will probably go to sleep as soon as they serve us our second dinner."

* * *

When they stepped out of the monstrous confusion of Charles de Gaulle airport, they took a shuttle into the Hilton in central Paris. It was midday and raining.

"Paris is the only place where the rain is beautiful," said Meredith. "It smears the landscape like a Monet painting."

"I love this city," said Aubrey. "I must admit, I'm not sorry for the delay. This place has got to be healing." He took a deep breath.

Meredith said, "It's like stepping into a caress."

Aubrey was glad to see the wonder light up Meredith's face at the sight of familiar landmarks. There had been too much anxiety, too much fear in those eyes the past week.

But for a couple of days, they could relax.

* * *

Aubrey had insisted that Meredith take a nap once they reached their luxurious hotel. While she slept, he stepped out and wandered down the Champs Élysées until he found a small but elegant bakery where he enjoyed an espresso and croissant.

The rain was a gentle mist now. Being here was like a dream somehow. He gazed at the Arc d' Triomphe in the distance and thought, as he always did, of the Germans striding through it in 1940, celebrating the fall of Paris. He could not even imagine what a horrible day that must have been for the Parisians.

But nothing like the terrorizing siege of Sarajevo his mother had lived through. He realized he was steeling himself for his arrival there.

Paris!

Rebuking himself for his nerves, he forced himself to let go of his concerns if only for a couple of days. He breathed in the sweetness of the little café in the heart of the most beautiful city in the world. Taking a sip of his espresso, he felt its warmth seep deep into his bones, and his worries leave his body, carried away by the soft breeze of the overhead fan.

This was a city to nurture the soul.

Putting his earbuds in, Aubrey listened to Vivaldi. The composer must have been a happy man to have written such joyful music.

Music, light, water, air, such fundamental blessings. Together they brought a measure of comfort and peace. But, there was nothing intrinsically magic about any of them, really. It was what they symbolized to the human mind. The comfort of balance that existed in the universe. God's balance. He and only He was the author of true and lasting peace.

More often than not, that peace escaped Aubrey. But now it was important that they carry it with them, this peace and beauty. Bosnia was going to be a dark place, full of the evidence of man's ability to hate his fellow man because of his beliefs.

Standing, he paid his check, and then wandered back outside into the magic cityscape. People scurried all around him. The ever-present honking horns accompanied the traffic that hurled down the avenue. Throwing back his head, he looked up at the now azure sky. The rain with its clouds had left, and the late afternoon sun was shining. He would go back to the hotel and bring Meredith out here to enjoy the Parisian light. Maybe if she could stay here long enough the brilliant city could heal her mind and heart.

He saw her face in his mind. It was thinner than it had been before she had left for Africa. But she was not emaciated. Instead, she looked fragile. *Handle with care.*

Aubrey wished Meredith could let go and be healed of whatever haunted her. Whatever had happened to her in the Mideast, it had so seared her heart that he was certain she believed she could never love again.

* * *

Meredith took him to a bistro in Les Halles that evening, telling him it had the best onion soup in Paris.

He shared with her the insight he had had that afternoon. "We need to take the loveliness and grace of Paris with us to Bosnia and pray it will inoculate us against the strife there."

To his chagrin, the light in her eyes faded, and there in the comfortable surroundings of the bistro, she began to look around as though she were trapped. She reached for her bag and pulled out her hand sanitizer.

"Calm down," he said. "What are you afraid of?"

"I *am* scared. Scared to death. I didn't realize it until now."

He drew his brows together. "Duric isn't going to appear suddenly in this bistro."

"Duric isn't what I'm afraid of."

Aubrey put a hand over hers. "Talk to me, Meredith."

"It's all about people killing each other because of their beliefs."

Through his mind raced all the things he thought he knew of Meredith—she was a fanatically hard worker, she proceeded with her duty in the face of her fears, but something tortured her. Something so deep she never spoke of it. This sudden anxiety of hers was a clue.

"Someone you were close to was killed because of their beliefs?" he asked.

She looked down, spreading her hands and then clutching them into fists full of sand. Tears spilled over and slid down her face. "Tell me," he said.

"My fiancé."

His mind flew over the facts he knew about her life. *No fiancé. She must have fallen in love in Africa. Or the Middle East.*

"You met him abroad?"

Meredith nodded, scrambling for a tissue.

"Here. Let me," he handed her the clean bandana handkerchief he carried in his jeans. "Go on," he said.

As she mopped her face, she said, "Some radical Muslims kidnapped him from the Christian refugee camp where we were." She stopped, the tears coming faster.

He guessed the rest. "They beheaded him."

She nodded. "There was never a kinder, more loving man."

"Those radical Muslims use Allah as an excuse to do violence. It's the West they hate," Aubrey said gently.

"I have given up trying to understand how their minds work. But I am afraid, Aubrey."

"Afraid to go to Bosnia?"

"Yes. There are a lot of Muslims there. And for them, the war twenty-five years ago was a Holy War."

"You're right. But things are different now. They live in peace with their Christian neighbors."

"All it would take is an incident—one anti-Muslim incident staged by someone as warped as Zoran Duric—and the killing could start all over again."

Aubrey felt her fear like a tentacle reaching out to grab him. He struggled for some perspective. "If terrorists mess with your mind and interfere with your objectives, then they have succeeded. We cannot live out our lives in fear."

"What then?" she asked, her face a mask of misery.

"As the British would say, we carry on. We do our bit. And in this case, our bit is to stop Zoran Duric."

He held out his fist. She straightened up and made a fist of her own. They bumped them together.

* * *

The next day they spent in the Louvre followed by a walk down by the Seine. It was cool, but sunny. They sat on a bench on the Pont Neuf looking at the Notre Dame. They took apples out of a string bag he carried and crunched on them.

"I can't believe we're here," she said.

Meredith wore olive green capris and a maize-colored blouse. Her hair was on top of her head in a messy bun. Even in her casual clothes, she looked like a fashionista.

"So," she said. "We take off tomorrow."

Anxious to avoid another meltdown, he said, "You know, I don't even know where you sprouted," Aubrey said. "Or why you chose to study Balkan history and politics of all things."

She took a bite of her apple and chewed before answering. "I grew up in Atlanta. My dad always worked for CNN as a foreign correspondent, so he was gone a lot. First in Bosnia and Kosovo, then in the Middle East. He talked a lot about the fall of the Wall and the break-up of Yugoslavia and the Soviet Union. How it was the defining event of the late 20th century."

Aubrey scooted his seat around the table, further in her direction. "I can see how that would be fascinating. Did you ever travel there?"

"I went to Belgrade and Zagreb when I was touring Europe during the summer between my sophomore and junior years. Never Sarajevo, though. I always thought that it was probably just a pile of rubble."

"Yeah. Me, too. But I was always curious. My mom loved Sarajevo and its mix of history and cultures when she was growing up there."

"I've seen pictures of the rubble. It is so sad."

"Then it will be good for you to see its rebirth. The Bosnians as a whole are a resilient people."

"I still have jet lag," said Meredith when they rose to go back to the hotel. "That's a pretty nice restaurant in the Hilton. Let's eat there tonight. Then I want to go to bed early to try to reset my clock."

CHAPTER TEN

Meredith went through an entire bottle of hand sanitizer on the 5-hour flight which included a stop in Zagreb. There was no doubt she was anxious.

But this was her life, her story. She needed to make the most of it.

"After Sarajevo, I think we need to head to the Drina River valley and a town called Zvornik," said Aubrey. "It's in the northeast and was probably where the worst of the Serbian ethnic cleansing took place in spring of 1992."

"The Drina marks the border with Serbia, right?"

"Yeah. And despite the war crimes, the Dayton Peace gave the Bosnian Serbs what they wanted."

"Yeah. Republika Srpska."

"Anything less than their own country would have probably extended the war."

"Agreed."

Finally, Meredith was so nervous she asked the flight attendant for a pack of cards. They played gin rummy for the rest of the flight.

* * *

Sarajevo wasn't exactly what she expected. It bustled, its thoroughfares crammed with people and their string shopping bags. The buildings were a mishmash of Roman, medieval, Ottoman, and modern. There was a proliferation of mosques with their minarets sailing over the city. She counted one synagogue, and many Catholic and Eastern Orthodox churches.

The war that was so much on her mind might never have happened. They checked into the Hotel President in the Old City. It had a terrace with views of Sarajevo. Meredith was pleased to see bridges and fountains and people. She heard the Muslim afternoon call to prayer which was both eerie and enchanting.

"The first thing we need to do is to get in touch with my mother's cousin, Bilijana Jovanovic," said Aubrey. "Mom called her and told her we were coming. She teaches English in a private school. She will know all about the family black sheep."

Meredith took a deep breath. "I'll do a quick charge on my phone while you call."

Aubrey's cousin lived in a modern apartment overlooking a greenspace filled with children and old people. Her space was small, but airy, light, and filled with bright colors.

She was a plump woman whose face still showed traces of the beauty she had once been. Though her hair was gray, she had the Slavic high cheekbones and large eyes that distinguished Aubrey's face. She smiled and kissed Stana's son on both cheeks. She hugged Meredith.

"Welcome! Come inside. I have tea or coffee, and I just went down to my bakery on the corner and bought a cake."

She remarked on Aubrey's similarity to his mother. She was full of family news and wanted to know all about Aubrey and when he was going to get married and give Stana grandchildren.

"Um," said Aubrey, clearly thrown off his stride, "We don't marry so young in America. At least not my generation."

Meredith laughed at his discomfiture. Then, to get him off the hook, she said, "Did Stana tell you we came to find out what you know of her brother, Zoran Duric?"

This chased the smile from her face. "We don't utter his name in my house."

"Do you know if there is a record anywhere of his war crimes?" asked Meredith. "My father was also in this country during the war, and he knew of him."

"The Bosniaks would have kept one. We try to forget."

Bosniaks, Meredith knew, were Muslim Bosnians.

"Is there someone we could interview, who could be a witness at his trial?" asked Aubrey. "He has been seen in Chicago, and I am worried for my mother. And for Meredith. She has received threats." He told her about the anonymous call and their research. "The only way to end all of this is to bring him to justice."

"It is thought that he is dead!"

"No. He's not," said Aubrey. "My mother said he had a child. Do you know what happened to it?"

"The Bosniaks were seeking justice as well. They killed the boy in some gruesome way. Some say Zoran was wounded at Zvornik and could never have another."

Aubrey took a small three by five tablet out of his shirt pocket. "What are some of the Bosniak names you can give me?"

She rattled off several names with no vowels that Meredith could hear, but she did recognize Ibram Ibrisimovic. Aubrey wrote them down along with the name of the Old Town mosques they probably attended.

"You must be prepared for some anger and suspicion. You have the look of your mother's brother, unfortunately."

"Oh!" exclaimed Meredith. "How unfortunate."

* * *

Thus began the grueling business of seeking out interviews that took place in coffee houses, tobacco shops, tea rooms, and on park benches. Meredith video-recorded them all and came to be exceedingly glad she did not speak Serbo-Croatian as Aubrey did.

At night, he was haunted by the things he heard that day. He listened to music from his playlist—lots of Bach—and had her tell him stories from her childhood. She told him of Brownies, Girl Scouts, her first-grade teacher, the Dad's show at her elementary school, her favorite books—Nancy Drew, Anne of Green Gables, and the Madeleine L'Engle series. And they talked baseball, lots of baseball as he was a White Sox fan, despite his move to the North Side and she was a die-hard Cubs fan.

She massaged his neck, and using the microwave in his room, made his mother's hot drink to soothe him. Meredith suspected, however, that he slept little.

Then came the day everything changed. They were holding interviews in an old abandoned stone schoolhouse. Aubrey told her his last interview hadn't shown up.

"I'm worried," he said. "The man who just left told me he thought he saw Duric in the marketplace. Something feels off."

Then Meredith felt it, too. A thick, pregnant silence hung in the cold, stone room.

Suddenly, a frightened woman came running into the school. Her eyes were round with terror.

She yelled something which only Aubrey could understand before she fled. He pulled Meredith to her feet, and they rushed out of the building just as it exploded. The shock waves threw them meters away from the burning ruin. Everyone in the street was screaming. Blackness overtook her.

The next thing Meredith knew, Aubrey was cradling her in his arms as he walked through a hospital. Her shoulder hurt like a hundred devils were trying to wrench her arm from its socket.

"What happened?" she asked, her brain fuzzy.

"Bomb," said Aubrey. "A Bosniak woman risked her life to warn us. We got out just in time, but we were thrown by the explosion. What hurts?"

A bomb! Her heart sped with adrenaline and fear. "My shoulder. I think I just wrenched it when I landed. How can you be so cool about this? We were almost killed!"

They finally reached the ER, and a nurse in a hijab spoke swiftly to Aubrey. She took Meredith's vitals, stitched and bandaged a cut on her forehead, and left, apparently telling Aubrey that a doctor would be in shortly.

"I should have warned you of the risk," said Aubrey. "But I thought you knew and were just playing it cool. There is more present-day unrest here than I expected. The people I have interviewed tell me that the Serbs are still threatening the Bosniaks and Croatians because they feel they are insufficiently recognized in the government. The only reason war has not broken out is because of EUFOR—the European Union's peacekeepers."

Fortunately, the doctor in the green scrubs who entered spoke English. He was short, swarthy, and all business.

"It is your shoulder?" he asked.

She winced as he explored it with his fingers. "Yes. I think it is probably dislocated."

"We will have an x-ray, before anything else. I don't want to injure you further."

Aubrey held her hand as the gurney took her to x-ray and when it was finished, all the way back to her curtained cubicle.

"So the peacekeepers—they are the guys in the blue berets we see in the street?" she asked.

"Yeah, I'm sorry. I should have left you with Bilijana."

"No. I needed to be with you. I needed to video everyone who spoke. It's important to have a visual for the story."

"I wouldn't have had you hurt for the world."

"I am going to be fine, Aubrey. Don't worry. But that was close. Do you think this story is worth our lives?"

"Probably not. But if we can get Zoran Duric, it will save many lives. He is worse than a wild animal. And that is slandering animals."

The adrenaline drained from her body, and suddenly exhaustion claimed her. She dozed. After what seemed like hours, the doctor returned and told her she was right about her shoulder.

"I can manipulate it back into place, but it would be very painful. I would rather do it under anesthetic."

"Yes," said Meredith. "I would prefer that."

He left again, and the nurse came back, had her sign a consent form that she couldn't read, and wheeled her up to the operating theater. Aubrey never left her side.

When she emerged from the anesthetic, he was there holding her hand.

"How is it?" he asked.

"It still hurts, but not like it did." She moved her arm up and down. "I'm going to be fine. How soon can we leave here? Bilijana must be terribly worried. I'm certain she heard about the explosion."

"I phoned her while you were under the anesthetic. She wants us to go to my Great Aunt Anastasijia's in Votopad while EUFOR investigates. She will send them out there to interview us. She is also sending all of our things to us here at the hospital. Her building is being watched by two men in a black car. EUFOR is going to arrest them."

"Is Votopad where you were born?" Right now she didn't feel like she wanted to go anywhere.

"Yes. Literally, it means waterfall. It's quite isolated. My great aunt lives in the house I was born in. Miraculously, nothing terrible happened in Votopad during the war. The Serbian agitators won't expect us to be there interviewing anyone."

Meredith was glad to see the rest of her clothes and toiletries. There was also a note for her from Aubrey's cousin.

Dear Meredith,

I cannot tell you how sorry I am for what has happened. I thank God for the woman who risked her life to warn you. The work you are doing is important, but not as important as your life. I pray you will convince Aubrey to take you home to the States.

You are a lovely pair. I hope someday to dance at your wedding.

With hope and thanks,

Bilijana

Meredith teared up at the words. Her emotions must be very close to the surface.

After dressing in jeans and a turtleneck top, she managed with her sore shoulder to get her hair into a ponytail. Aubrey came into her cubicle and spirited her and all of their gear out a staff entrance in the back of the hospital where he had a rental car waiting.

Night had fallen. Bilijana had sent apples and pastries from her bakery which they ate as they drove. As they traveled down roads full of potholes and erosion, Meredith directed Aubrey using the map on her phone. Other than that, she was too exhausted for talking.

At ten o'clock, they arrived at the little cottage of the elderly great aunt whose address Stana had given them before they left.

So this is where Aubrey was born.

Unfortunately, the village was so small it did not even have street lights, so they had used a flashlight from the glove compartment to find the house. Aubrey's mother had deeded the cottage to her aunt when she left for America.

Aunt Anastasijia was very happy to see them. She gave them dinner, hot baths, and warm beds. Unfortunately for Meredith, she had no English.

Her home was a bit like a fairy-tale dollhouse made of ancient stone with white plaster walls and exposed beams. Everything was scrubbed clean which Meredith was happy to see. Woven rugs in bright colors covered the tile floors, and the furniture was made of sturdy oak.

Meredith realized she hadn't used her hand sanitizer once since the bombing. After remedying that, she fell into her bed and covered herself with a bright red and blue quilt. In spite of the pain in her shoulder, she went right to sleep.

In the morning, after Aubrey enjoyed a pleasant conversation with his great aunt, they took off on foot to see the waterfalls. With their white, lacy falls of water from several different heights into the blue-green pool below, they were spectacular—one of the most beautiful sights in Europe, according to Aunt Anastasijia. Next to the gigantic falls, surrounded by ancient cliffs and trees, Meredith felt minuscule.

How many times over the centuries had this land been sacked, burned, and its people brutalized? She and Aubrey were chronicling only a tiny amount of the suffering this country had seen.

She spoke her thoughts to Aubrey.

"Yeah. EUFOR has eight hundred troops deployed here. But I am finding out there are acts of violence all the time."

Meredith shivered.

Aubrey put his arm around her as he said, "My cousin is sending their commanding officer to talk to us. EUFOR needs to know about Zoran Duric if they don't already."

Meredith was confused. "You think he is behind the bombing?"

"I think he heard about us through his grapevine. He must know we have more than enough evidence to cook his goose."

"So you think he is here now?"

"I haven't any idea. It depends on why he went to Chicago. He's not a terrorist out of Serbian displeasure over a peace that didn't go the way he wanted it to. He is motivated by hate, and he must hate that my mother married an American. He must hate that she has a son and he never will."

"You think he went there to kill you?"

"If he somehow found out where we were. Maybe he just went to Chicago because it has always been a destination for Serbian immigrants. He doesn't know our names. But he got a spot of luck when the anonymous caller got you involved. If he's seen me with you, he's got to know I'm his nephew. I look just like my grandfather, my mom says."

"You know what?" Meredith said. "We should just go back to Paris and stay there."

"I don't blame you for feeling that way. But my cousin's in danger because of me, and my mother is, too. We've got to corner this guy somehow. If not here, then in Chicago."

Meredith was sick at heart. "There is so much beauty in this country, why do they tear each other to pieces? I'm so sorry I ever got you involved in this. And your mother and cousin. And now your great aunt."

"I'm not. This guy has got to be taken down. The world has to see that things are different now. That such barbaric acts as Duric has committed will not be tolerated. That individuals will be held accountable even if they were members of a mob."

"Surely we have enough now to put the man away for several lifetimes," she said to Aubrey.

"In Sarajevo, he was not the ringleader. But in Zvornik he was. I think we need to travel there and document his deeds."

She sighed from deep within herself. "I guess it is an unexpected move on our part, so maybe we can get away with it."

"It will give us both a chance to see more of the country. My phone says that Zvornik is only two and a half hours away. The road is good, and the scenery will be memorable, I'm sure. We'll go as soon as we've spoken to the EUFOR guy."

* * *

Major General Anton Waldner of EUFOR came to the cottage the next day with his driver.

"Your cousin tells me you have been collecting evidence from the Bosniaks about Zoran Duric," the officer said after they were seated with cups of tea around the tiny table in Aunt Anastasijia's cottage.

"Yes," said Meredith. "We are journalists." She told him about the anonymous caller and the threats she had received in Chicago after she started trying to locate him.

Aubrey said, "He is also my uncle and has a vendetta against my mother and me who are now US citizens. We figured the only way to stop him was to get the FBI after him, but they weren't interested in crimes that were now over twenty-five years old. We've been operating alone."

"Duric's crimes did not end with the war," said the Major General. Using his sleeve, he wiped the sweat from his brow, though the day was not warm. "He is a deadly agitator still. He seems to be fueled by pure hatred."

The soldier brought a picture up on his phone. "I will send these to you. They are pictures of him planting the bomb in that schoolhouse. One of our confidential informants has been following him since he arrived back in the country a couple of days ago. If we can bring him in here in Bosnia, we will do so. However, if he escapes back to the States, the FBI can use this as current evidence against him."

Meredith and Aubrey looked at the picture. It clearly showed Duric's face with its high forehead and roman nose. His mouth, generous and wide, was Aubrey's mouth, and they shared a square jaw, but their noses were different. And Aubrey still had all his hair.

"So, he is here," said Meredith, feeling suddenly vulnerable in a way she never had in Chicago.

"We will do our best to capture him. Kettering, your cousin says you have plenty of evidence to try him here. We will try to get him imprisoned for the rest of his life."

Meredith didn't know why the soldier's promise didn't comfort her.

Maybe because I have experienced Duric's hatred first hand. I don't think he can be easily contained. His feelings burn too strong. They consume everything in their path.

Aubrey and Meredith gave him their email addresses, and the Major General sent them the picture.

His face was rigid with tension. "I advise you to get back to Chicago. Duric has too many lieutenants around here that are anxious to do his bidding," the soldier said. "He is like quicksilver. He keeps slipping through our fingers."

"He must have a secret bolt hole. He's eluded capture for twenty-five years," said Aubrey.

"We've discovered that he spent most of that time living in Vienna. He has only returned to become a thorn in our sides recently," said the major general.

"Now that Meredith is feeling better, we are going to take a short trip to Zvornik to gather some more direct evidence. Duric was a leader in the atrocities there. Then we will return to Sarajevo and be on our way back to the States. We have what we came for."

"You are journalists and have already proved yourselves to be a high-profile target. I must insist that you accept a EUFOR escort to Zvornik."

"It will only call attention to us," said Aubrey.

"That's what we're after. We want men like Duric to realize you are not an easy target. If he is determined to take you out, he's going to go, too."

Meredith touched Aubrey's rigid arm. "The major general is right, Aubrey. We will be much safer with an escort."

"You are my responsibility," insisted the EUFOR soldier. We can't afford to have an incident where you are concerned. It could escalate into another war."

"All right," Aubrey agreed finally. "But separate vehicles."

"Right. One before and one behind. We don't want you ambushed."

Meredith felt a whole lot better about the trip to Zvornik.

CHAPTER ELEVEN

While they waited for the EUFOR escort to arrive, Aubrey took Meredith for one more visit to the glorious waterfall.

"The major general seemed determined. Are you hopeful that EUFOR will be able to capture Duric?" she asked as she watched the iconic waterfall.

"Not very, I'm afraid. And I don't much like going back to Chicago under these uncertain circumstances, but we have a job to do. Now that we have a decent picture of the man, I have an idea," he said.

"We can do the exposé and ask for the public's help in catching him," Meredith guessed.

"Exactly. If he is unwise enough to return to our beloved city."

They were quiet for a few minutes, letting the falls work their magic. "This is such a romantic spot," Meredith said. "It seems all wrong to be discussing Duric here."

"I would much rather kiss you," said Aubrey, his face straight so she couldn't tell whether he was teasing. "But I know you wouldn't welcome it."

Her feelings were unexpectedly torn. Deep inside, she had warmth and something else rising perilously close to her heart. Meredith pushed it down and stood.

"Shall we see if we can walk behind that fall over there?" she asked.

"You know you have feelings for me," he said with a slow grin.

"Self-confidence has sure never been your problem," she returned. "I'm going for a walk."

"I had better come with you in case you need to be rescued. I make a heck of a white knight."

"With all that armor, you'd drown," she said.

He laughed.

One could, in fact, walk behind the waterfall. It was an enchanted fairyland with a huge sheet of water cutting off the rest of the world. Aubrey pulled her to his side with an arm around her waist. Turning, he just kissed her temple.

She did not pull away.

This waterfall has a mischievous sprite who is conspiring against me.

Her heart beat a happy tattoo, and suddenly it was all Meredith could do to keep from throwing herself into Aubrey's arms.

But she didn't want to give him the wrong idea.

* * *

The road to Zvornik was heavily wooded and wound through rising elevations. Meredith read the online travel literature. Before and after them were armored Jeeps, giving her a sense of safety.

"I know we're not here as tourists, but there's a twelfth-century fortress that looks across the river to Serbia. Looks like it's been an embattled border town for hundreds of years."

"It's kind of weird to realize this country's history is my history," said Aubrey.

"It must be," she said. "My lineage is boring. All northwestern European."

"We Slavs are tempestuous and irresistible."

"No comment," she said.

As they descended into the valley of the Drina river, they saw a montage of red-tiled old buildings and were surprised by all the modern high rises.

"With the river winding through like that, it looks lovely," said Meredith. "So hard to conceive that more lives were lost here than anywhere but Sarajevo."

"Yes. And a master terrorist was my Uncle Zoran," Aubrey said, his voice heavy.

Meredith patted his hand on the wheel. There didn't seem to be anything to say to that.

For a while, Meredith said nothing, but the further they drove into the town, the more uncomfortable she became, despite their escort.

"Call me crazy, but I'm not getting a good vibe from this place. I think we should record this guy you've lined up and then get out before sundown," said Meredith.

"If that's what you want, fine. I can't say I'm crazy about it either." He reached into his breast pocket. "There's the address Ibrisimovic gave me for his brother. I already gave it to the EUFOR guys, so I guess we just follow them."

"What makes a Bosniak stay in a place like this after such a massacre?" she asked.

"It's his family home. Has been for two hundred years. It's supposed to be really something."

They followed the jeep in front of them through the town and up the far mountainside until they reached a red-tile-roofed villa.

"This is quite a place. Look at all that beautiful white and blue figured tile. Very Ottoman. But still spooky," said Meredith.

They parked their rental in the circular drive and got out. The military escort in the front car, got out, too. Meredith stretched her legs by bending over at the waist and touching the gravel. She whisked out her hand sanitizer and rubbed in a drop.

Then they walked to the door, the escort preceding them and checking out the area. No one responded to their knock. After a few minutes, Aubrey used the ornate brass knocker again. The door was opened by a little woman hunched with age and dressed as a servant. She had been crying and held a handkerchief up to her cheek.

After wailing a few words, she shut the door in their faces.

Meredith looked at Aubrey. "What on earth did she say?"

"Mr. Ibrisimovic was murdered last night," he replied, his voice low. "We're out of here right now."

One of their military escorts, a tall redhead, heard him, and Meredith listened as he radioed in the information. He requested a crime unit to come in and process the site. As four soldiers were riding in each vehicle, the redhead instructed two of them to remain at the site.

Then he said, "Someone knew you were coming. They could have prepared an ambush. We are going to go back to Sarajevo a different way. It is longer, and when the sun goes down we will have to stop. Without waiting for their response, the soldier climbed into his vehicle.

Aubrey's tires spun on the gravel and finally lurched forward down the drive. Meredith sat like a stone, trying to take in what had happened.

They took a road which wasn't much more than a track. "This isn't a four-wheel drive," said Aubrey. "It's going to be slow-going."

Soon they connected with a secondary road which was marginally better. Aubrey said, "Someone has figured out how to track us. First, the school explodes while we're there, and now Ibrisimovic's brother is killed before we can talk to him."

"Poor Mr. Ibrisimovic! He was murdered because we were going to talk to him. It's our fault, Aubrey!"

"No. The fault lies with Duric, if I'm not mistaken."

"But he wouldn't have had him killed if we hadn't made an appointment with him."

"I know," said Aubrey, his words dropping like a stone into a well.

Silence fell on the little car, and Meredith tried to deal with her feelings of guilt. They wouldn't go away. The scenery on this road didn't look nearly as charming as it had coming the other way.

There was nothing charming about this country! For centuries it had been embattled. This corner of the world was drenched in blood. As for Duric, that one man had the kind of hatred and psychosis to plunge the whole country back into war.

Suddenly, her whole body rebelled.

"Pull over, Aubrey," she said. "I'm going to be sick."

She managed to contain her nausea until there was enough of a shoulder for him to park the car off the road. Meredith opened the car door, got out and raced into the trees where she was violently ill. She was so weak; she could no longer stand. Walking back to the car was too much for her. Halfway there, her knees gave way, and she collapsed onto a fallen log.

Aubrey was beside her in an instant. Behind him walked the tall red-headed soldier. "What's happening here?" he demanded.

"You aren't needed," said Aubrey, his voice sharp with irritation. "She's been sick."

"I'm sorry," she said, rubbing her arms as she trembled. "All this violence is just getting to me. I guess I need a time out."

Aubrey sat beside her and pulled her to him. "Do you want to stop for the day? There was a sign back there. It looks like there's a village coming up."

"Would EUFOR mind?"

"I don't care what they say. We're stopping."

"Well, I think I had better. I'm sorry to be such a weak-kneed idiot." She cringed at her own words. "I'm usually stronger than this."

"So am I," he said. "Neither of us is used to this level of violence."

"How did Duric know we were going to see Ibrisimovic's brother?"

"The guy is an evil genius, it seems."

"I'm frightened, Aubrey. He wants us dead, too."

"That's why we're going to go home. But I do think we need a timeout, as you said. We need to make a plan. It was my idea to go to Zvornik. I should have known we were running into danger."

"Let's go to the village," she said. "Just now, I want to be off the grid."

"We're hardly going to be that. EUFOR isn't exactly invisible. Have you got your strength back?"

"Yes. I'll be fine now."

* * *

To Aubrey's surprise, the red-headed soldier agreed that an unscheduled stop at a remote village was a good idea. "We don't want to alarm the residents, though. They're touchy in Republika Srpska about our presence in their country. I'll wire you for sound if you don't mind. We'll be parked just out of town. I'm giving you a radio, too, in case you need to get hold of us. But we'll be monitoring you. Code word: 'dangerous.' If we hear you say that, we're coming in."

Aubrey agreed and was fitted out with the transponding wire before they drove off.

The village was tiny, nestled amid the forest in a small valley. The houses were made of stone with red-tiled roofs. The largest building was a tidy domed Orthodox church in the center. A neat little coffee bar sat near it, next to the post office. Mostly filled with old men smoking pipes, it was dim inside, with a glass case filled with baked goods next to the register. The aroma of coffee was welcoming.

Meredith sat at the one empty wooden table and took out her hand sanitizer. She felt like she needed to bathe in it but settled for using it on her hands and face and the back of her neck. When she finished, she realized all the men were staring at her. She gave them a shaky smile.

Aubrey brought her hot cocoa and a pastry. "I didn't think coffee would be good for your stomach at the moment," he said. "And it would be good for you to have something soothing. Cocoa and pastry fit the bill."

All at once, she was ravenous. By the time Aubrey returned with his own snack, she had eaten half of what she had decided was a cream horn. The cocoa was rich and not too sweet.

"They have figured out that we're Americans," he said.

"This is nice," she said. "I wonder if there's anywhere we can stay."

"Let's just let them get used to us. Then I'll ask."

Before too long, Aubrey had engaged a few of the men in conversation. They were delighted that he spoke their language. Soon they were talking and laughing.

Meredith sipped her cocoa and felt herself relax. There was no way that Duric could find them here. And there was EUFOR. There appeared to be only one way in and out of this village. And the jeeps were there, just out of sight.

Around four o'clock the men began starting for home. Aubrey had been keeping her in the loop, telling her that he explained that his "wife" wasn't well, and was there any place they could stay for the night. "There was no other way I could think to describe why we were traveling together in such a remote area," he apologized.

"Did they have a place?"

"Several of the men invited us to stay."

In the end, there was only one man left. He was a jolly type, smiling at her happily. According to Aubrey, he was to be their host.

His cottage was only a short walk down the street. Made of grayish white river rocks, it had a green door and shutters. As they walked inside, Meredith saw that it was neat and comfortable looking. A woman she took to be the man's wife stood in the open kitchen stirring what smelled like a stew.

There was an exchange between husband and wife. The woman came out to them, smiling and chattering to Aubrey like a long-lost relative. Soon she led Meredith and Aubrey to a small room where there were twin beds covered by colorful crazy quilts. He translated the information that it was their children's old room and left with their hostess, so Meredith could rest.

Before long, she fell into a heavy sleep.

* * *

Dinner that evening was a simple lamb and vegetable stew with large white biscuits. Meredith felt as though she had wandered into a fairy tale. She couldn't imagine living in a village such as this, spending her days cooking and cleaning and visiting with the same small band of neighbors, day after day. Right now, it seemed like it would be a charmed existence. Why had she made her life so complicated?

Aubrey helped teach her a Serbian card game that turned out to be a version of Hearts. They played among much laughter.

Meredith was drawn to the couple who seemed neither old nor young. Spiridon was the postmaster for the town. He and Ana had two grown children who lived in Zvornik. Their daughter was a nurse and their son an auto mechanic. They were both married with babies on the way. The couple was thrilled that they would soon be grandparents.

Meredith and Aubrey retired at ten o'clock when their hosts said good night.

"It feels like we've found a little bit of heaven," she said when they were settled for the night in their twin beds. "Thank you for suggesting that we stop here."

"It is nice," he said. "I can't even imagine what life in such a place would be like, but I expect both of us would have moved on to a city if we had grown up in such a place."

"You're probably right. We weren't made for tranquility."

All the same, Meredith found herself saying a private prayer that night, thankful for their island of peace.

"I want to go home, Aubrey," she said the next morning when they were back in their car headed down the road. "That murder is as good as an indictment of Duric's guilt. We have everything we need for the FBI and our story."

"I agree. But I have to tell our Mr. Ibrisimovic what has happened to his brother. I somehow doubt that EUFOR has told him anything, but even if they have, we owe it to him to offer our condolences. He has been a huge help to us. Would you mind texting him to meet us at the Hotel President lobby? I know we have already checked out, but I don't want to endanger Bilijana."

"He speaks English?"

"Yes. Very well."

Meredith sent the text.

CHAPTER TWELVE

When Aubrey and Meredith arrived at the hotel, the redheaded officer and one other soldier followed them in.

"I thought you would be headed for the airport," he said.

"We are meeting our informant here. It was his brother that was killed in Zvornik. We want to offer our condolences. Then we're off for the airport."

"My instructions are to escort you to the airport and aboard your plane. Two of us will cover you here in the lobby, while the rest of us will be waiting in our vehicles around the corner."

Aubrey gave a short nod. He would be extremely glad when they left his scarred birthplace behind.

He and Meredith found a cozy corner where there were sofas set up opposite one another before a hearth with a fire.

Ibram Ibrisimovic entered, and Aubrey waved him over to where they were sitting. A short man in Western clothing with a full black beard, he smiled as he saw them. Aubrey felt a sudden pang of grief. How could he tell this man his awful news?

"Was my brother able to help you?" the Bosniak asked.

"Mr. Ibrisimovic, I have some very bad news," Aubrey paused, hesitant to go on. The man who sat next to him frowned. "We didn't get to see your brother. A servant told us he had been murdered. I think she was the only one in the house. EUFOR is on the scene and handling it. I am certain they will be in touch with you. Meredith and I are so very sorry for your loss."

Ibrisimovic jumped to his feet, his hands clenched. Throwing back his head, he emitted a roar of rage.

Suddenly, Aubrey heard someone scream outside the hotel. Acting on pure instinct, he pulled Meredith down with him to the floor. A cacophony of shots crashed through the hotel lobby traveling from one end to the other, smashing the glass front doors and windows, the lights, the check-in desk. Their informant ducked and threw himself down next to them.

"Duric!" he yelled.

The shots came again, moving back through the lobby. A muscle engine revved and the death car screamed down the street and away.

Instantly, Aubrey was on his feet checking out the lobby for injuries. Their informant was unharmed but white with shock. The clerk behind the desk was not visible. Two people lay on the floor, too still. One of the EUFOR men was down. The other rushed toward them.

"This way," the man commanded them.

They followed him out a side door of the hotel, straight to the waiting vehicles. Fortunately, they had their money and passports in money belts around their waists. Meredith clutched their computer which they had been afraid to leave in their car.

Her eyes were large with shock, and they were both shaking. He saw that there were glass bits in her hair. After dispatching four of the soldiers back into the hotel, the EUFOR officer helped them into the Jeep. They sped through the streets, a klaxon sounding over their head. In what seemed like minutes they heard helicopters above them.

Holding Meredith's cold hand, Aubrey checked out the back window to see the traffic jam that was unfolding. That was in their favor. No one could get through it to follow them.

The airport seemed only a short distance outside Sarajevo. When they had reached it, both soldiers in the vehicle accompanied them in. They walked, four abreast with the soldiers carrying assault weapons, to the terminal departures screen.

A plane to Amsterdam would leave in twenty minutes. They could just make it.

* * *

As soon as they were aboard the plane, Aubrey let out a heavy sigh and said, "I'm emailing Bilijana right now to let her know we are okay and what we are doing."

"I hope we haven't put her in danger," Meredith said. She was furiously scrubbing herself with hand sanitizer. "Aubrey! We were nearly killed. Those poor people in the lobby! I wish we knew what happened to them. And Mr. Ibrisimovic. I think he was going into shock."

"EUFOR will have called an ambulance."

The adrenaline rush was passing off now that they were in the air, and Aubrey began to shake—hard and brutal jolts. Meredith was trembling, too. He watched as tears fell down her face, and a wave of sorrow washed over him.

"How did Duric always know exactly what we were doing?" she asked.

"I've been thinking about that. I should have been onto him sooner. My guess is he cloned Ibrisimovic's phone. His phone wasn't safe. We'd better dump our phones, too. We can leave them on the airplane."

Meredith was very white and had bitten her lip so hard it was bleeding.

Taking her hand, he said, "Honey, it's over. It's behind us. We're safe."

She silently passed him her hand sanitizer. "Who knows what germs we picked up on that floor?"

He stared at her and then laughed, but it sounded more like a croak.

* * *

Schiphol airport was a welcome sight.

"Do you want to spend the night in Amsterdam?" he asked.

"Are there any flights tonight to O'Hare?"

They checked and saw that the next flight to Chicago was at 10 a.m. Aubrey bought their tickets, and they set off in search of a restaurant as they were both hungry.

Meredith pointed out a pub-like eatery that specialized in small meals and homey atmosphere for travelers who awaited flights.

"This is just right," Meredith said. After they were seated, she shook herself and said, "You know, we just lived through one heck of a story. Thank heavens for EUFOR."

"That's my girl," he said. "Glass half full."

"We had better see if we can buy some new phones somewhere and call Mr. Q. He is liable to think we're dead if he listens to the news."

"I doubt it will even make the news in the States," said Aubrey. "Everyone thinks these types of things are everyday occurrences in the Balkans."

Meredith shook herself again, and Aubrey noticed that her hand trembled as she reached for her cola.

After a couple of hours had passed and they had regained some sense of personal safety, Meredith said, "I always thought of the Balkans as a very Romantic place, in the literary and musical sense," she said. "My father loved the people there, even during the war. He said they never took life for granted and appreciated even small mercies like fresh vegetables. They loved much and fought hard."

"I think that's true. That certainly describes my mother."

She smiled at him. He knew he probably looked like he'd been in a fight. "Do you take after her or after your father?" she asked.

"If I took after my father, I would have been a lot more scholarly and less 'hands-on' about this story. That's the difference between a journalist and a professor."

"So, you love much and fight hard?" she asked, her voice teasing.

"I do, as a matter of fact. And I appreciate fresh vegetables like you wouldn't believe."

Before she could object, he leaned across the small table and kissed her.

Meredith sobered. "Aubrey. I know our emotions are on overdrive after what we have just been through, but I also know in some part of me that I'm still not in the market for romance. I've been hurt enough for one lifetime, and you are every bit as idealistic as Jan."

"Jan?"

"Remember?" she fired at him. "The man I loved with all my heart? The man who was killed?"

"Cool down. Of course, I remember. You just never told me his name." He frowned. After all they had just been through, he couldn't believe she didn't feel the closeness he felt. But, he would have to let her discover that. He couldn't talk her into it. He changed the subject. "So, you're not idealistic?"

The question apparently threw her. "I'm a practical coward," she said.

"Allow me to disagree. Do practical cowards even major in Balkan history and politics in the first place? What were you going to do with a major like that? Do practical cowards become investigative journalists? Go to Africa to report on the plight of the refugees? Do they put themselves in harm's way in order to take a dangerous sociopath off the streets?" He grinned at her. "No, and no, etcetera."

She relaxed back into her chair. "You got me." Reaching across the table, she took his hand. "But I guess I still need comfort like any other human being."

"I'm very good at comforting," he said.

* * *

After overnighting at the large airport Hilton, they flew business class heading for O'Hare. Though they hadn't had clean clothes, at least they had been able to shower. Aubrey guessed that Meredith had spent a long time washing away the horrors of the previous day and that putting on soiled clothing had made her feel that her life was out of control.

"I guess our first priority is getting this story written," said Meredith when they were eating their airline luncheon. "It will make a good feature story for the ten o'clock news. With our up-to-date picture of Duric, we should be able to solicit the public's help to find him, if he comes back to Chicago."

"I don't think for a moment that he has finished his business there. Something brought him to Chicago in the first place. Then, somehow, he stumbled across my family and me."

"I led him straight to you. But how did he know you were his nephew? You changed your names. And how did he find me in the first place? How did he know I was looking for him?"

"My mother has always told me I look just like her father, but we may never know how he got on to you. I think with his hatred of the Muslims, his business in Chicago has to do with the Islamic Cultural Center. Like I told you, it serves mostly Bosnian Muslims. From the way the Imam reacted to his name, I think they are personally acquainted from the war years. Maybe the Imam has something to do with the death of Ouric's son. Maybe he traced him to Chicago. Finding me was a bonus."

"I think we need to go straight to the FBI with all our new information," said Meredith. "It's time to take him down."

"I agree. He's a one-man war."

They began outlining the feature they were going to do, probably spread out over several broadcasts. They had downloaded the pictures they had taken of EUFOR onto their computer before they ditched their phones and bought new ones in Amsterdam.

"We had better call Mr. Q," she said finally. "I want to get on the ten o'clock news tonight. I know it's still night there, but he'll want to know."

Their boss was disoriented from sleep at first, but after they advised them that they were running from a drive-by shooting and had nearly been blown up on another occasion, he was fully alert and agreed that Meredith should do a story on the ten o'clock news. He also agreed to her desire to do an in-depth feature.

"I think it would be a good idea for you to send someone down to the Islamic Cultural Center in Northbrook to interview the Imam about this. We have already warned him about Duric. I think there is some personal history between them. We have a picture of Duric now which I will send you," said Meredith. "We need the public's help to find him. I'm sure he's on his way back to the US."

They were bone-deep tired after the eight-and-a-half-hour flight arrived in Chicago. It was only mid-afternoon Central Time which gave them plenty of time to write up their story. An Uber took them home to Meredith's condo.

"I've never been so happy to be home," she said. "I can't wait to take a bath and get out of these clothes. Then we can call the FBI."

"Go ahead and shower," he said. "I'll call Mr. Q to tell him we've landed."

Their boss was glad they were back in one piece.

"This Zoran Duric is determined to take out Meredith and me. I am going to talk to the FBI about a safe house."

"I don't like your risking your lives for a story," Mr. Q said. "Call the FBI."

"Hopefully, they'll cooperate. I imagine Meredith will want to work here in her condo this afternoon. We'll come in to the station after she gets her story filled in. We outlined it on the plane."

"Sounds good," said Mr. Q. "We'll see you in a bit."

After he disconnected, he could still hear Meredith's bath running, so he called his dad at his office.

"We're back, Dad," he said.

"Good. Did you have any trouble?"

"A bit," he said. "But we managed to make it out alive."

"I hope you're exaggerating," his dad said.

"Not much, actually. Listen, I'm sure Duric knows who I am if I look as much like my grandfather as Mom says. I think we should all go into a safe house if I can convince the FBI of the danger."

"Not a bad idea," his dad said. "I'll talk to your mother about it. I'll have to arrange for things here so that I can be gone."

"Believe me; this guy means business, Dad."

"Okay. Let me know."

When Meredith came out of her bedroom, dressed in a navy blazer suit with a cream turtleneck, he said, "Time to call the FBI."

"Do you mind if I finish my story, first? Why don't you go home and change and pick up something for us to eat while I work on finishing it up? Take my car."

"I hate leaving you alone."

"I have triple locks."

"I have my Glock at home. I'll pick that up. Come to the door with me. I want to hear you fasten those locks when I leave."

When she handed him her keys, she kissed him on the cheek. "Be careful."

* * *

Aubrey went home to Skokie, showered, shaved and dressed in khakis and a navy blue pullover. Then he drove back to Evanston, where he went to his favorite pancake place and bought a huge baked apple pancake to go.

By the time he got back to Meredith's, she'd finished her story and was ready to call the FBI. To his relief, no one had bothered her. He could only suppose Duric was still in Bosnia. Her eyes lit up at the sight of the apple pancake.

Their call to Assistant Special Agent in Charge Hamilton Werner went as well as could be expected.

"So, you were right about this Duric fellow. And now you expect him to follow you back to the States?" Werner asked.

"I think he has an agenda with the Islamic Cultural Center in Northbrook, as well as unfinished business with Ms. Montgomery and me and my family." He explained what they had not known when they had spoken to him last time, "My mother is his sister and they have a bitter history. He believes she betrayed him by marrying my father and coming to America, his enemy. As for Ms. Montgomery, she is airing a story on him tonight which will include an account of his attacks on us in Sarajevo." He remembered the pictures they had downloaded from their phones to their computer. "We now have a picture of him which she will broadcast, along with a tip line for people to call. We'd like them to be able to call the FBI direct. What telephone number should she use?"

Werner rattled off a number. "You are deliberately endangering yourselves."

"We were hoping you might have a safe house for all of us."

"How long do you have before this broadcast?"

Since the phone was on speaker, Meredith answered, "I have to be at the station by eight-thirty."

"Then you have time to come down to headquarters and give us a statement. I will need that and a print of that picture of Duric to make the arrangements for the safe house, but I agree that it is a good idea. "I'll brief Special Agent Marks. He'll be waiting for you. How soon can you get here?"

"We'll leave Evanston now."

As soon as he hung up, he called his father.

"Thank you for taking care of that, Aubrey. Now all I have to do is convince your mother if she ever gets home."

"She's not there?"

"No. I just got home from work. I'm sure she'll be home soon. There's something cooking in the Crock Pot."

"We'll call you back after we've heard what the FBI has to say."

They disconnected. Meredith came out of the bedroom with a suitcase. "I'm not going to be without a change of clothes again," she said.

"I suppose you remembered your hand sanitizer?"

"One big bottle and six little ones," she said.

"I'm glad to know you won't be caught off guard," he said. "Speaking of which, I've got my Glock."

"Good."

* * *

Special Agent Marks was a good-sized man with a strong grip when he shook Aubrey's hand. His partner, Special Agent Sandra Steele was an average-sized blonde who looked like a good wind would blow her over.

They both listened to Aubrey and Meredith's story with polite attention that became more marked the deeper they got into the tale.

"Yes. I think a safe house is definitely indicated. Especially after you make that broadcast. Can your parents meet us at the station afterward and we'll all go together? I'll need some time to organize this," said Agent Steele. "We need to put out a nationwide alert on this guy. The Chicago Police should also be brought into the picture."

"That will work well," said Meredith.

"I'll just call my folks," said Aubrey.

While he dialed, Meredith emailed the Special Agents the picture of Zoran Duric.

"Dad, I'm calling from FBI headquarters. We're on for the safe house."

"It may be a little late. I don't know how to tell you this, Aubrey, but your mother is missing."

* * *

Badly shaken, Aubrey reported his news to the FBI agents and Meredith.

"When did she go missing?" Meredith asked.

"Sometime today. She never came home, and she had dinner cooking."

"Oh, Aubrey! I'm so sorry. I thought we left all that behind. Duric didn't waste any time," said Meredith.

"Yeah. He didn't waste any time," said Aubrey, his words clipped as he tried to keep his emotions contained. "He must have gotten a midnight flight from Paris or London yesterday. I need to get home to my father."

"We'll take you," said Agent Marks. "While I drive, Agent Steele can finish making the arrangements for the safe house by phone. We'll also have the Chicago Police meet us at the house."

Meredith stepped up to Aubrey and put her hands on his chest, looking up into his eyes. "Aubrey, I know how close you are to your mother. I don't even know what to say."

Shock had numbed his brain. "I can't take it in. I feel so bad for my dad. He couldn't get in touch with us because he doesn't have a cell and he didn't have my new number. Stupidity on my part. The station didn't have it either."

"I wish I could go with you," Meredith said, "But I'll rewrite my story and your mom's kidnapping will be the lead. We'll get the public's help."

* * *

When they arrived at the Hyde Park house, he looked at it as though it were for the first time. For him, home had always been colored by his mother's presence. A fresh blow smote him.

She's not here. For the first time in my whole life, she's not here.

His father was in jeans and a University of Chicago sweatshirt, his hair looking as though he had been running hands through it. He took the agents into the kitchen and poured them bad coffee. The police arrived, but he was oblivious.

"When was the last time you talked to her?" he asked his dad.

"I haven't talked to her all day. Every time I called, she wasn't home."

"When was the earliest you called?" Aubrey asked.

"About eleven this morning. I wondered if she had heard anything from you. We were growing anxious."

Aubrey felt guilt gnaw at his gut. It had never occurred to him to keep his parents informed.

He turned to the agents. "I've been thinking. We need to find out how quickly Duric could have gotten here from Sarajevo. We got the first flight out after the shooting incident at the hotel. It went to Amsterdam. He wasn't on it. There wasn't a flight from Amsterdam to Chicago until today at ten. Unless he got some crazy fast connection from somewhere else, this might not have been Duric himself. He could have a confederate."

Then he smote his head. "Sorry. Dad, these are Special Agents Steele and Marks. Agents, this is my dad, Dr. William Kettering," said Aubrey. The police also introduced themselves.

"You know, the more I think about it, Dad, the more I wonder if he *is* working with someone else. That's a possibility that has never occurred to us before."

"If Duric is behind this, how did he ever find us?" asked his father. "We've changed our name. How did he even know we were in Chicago?"

Aubrey's brain felt sluggish, but he urged his thought processes on. "He knew Meredith and I were investigating him. Remember the threat she received?" A name burst into his mind. "Father Savic!" he said. "He was asking around the neighborhood to see if anyone else had seen Duric. It must have gotten back to Duric. He *must* have one or more confederates in this country. Especially if he's going to do a job of any size."

"So, you think Duric may have gotten one of them to take her?" his dad asked.

"It depends on what we find out about the flights."

"Do you have wi-fi?" asked Agent Steele.

Aubrey's dad said, "Yes. You can set up on the kitchen table, or I can take you back to my office. I'll give you my password."

"This will be fine."

After his father had taken care of this detail, Aubrey said, "You say I look just like mom's father, Dad. Once he saw me, he must have been over-the-moon pleased when he figured out that I was his nephew. He got my name from WOOT, I'm sure. As Meredith's colleague. When he had the name 'Kettering', he just googled you. You're all over the internet with your publications. He would have traced you to the University of Chicago without any problem. You're in the regular directory, right? It would have been easy to come up with your address. We have reason to know that he's tech-savvy."

"Okay," said Agent Steele. "The next flight out of Sarajevo after yours was to Vienna this morning. Flights from London and Paris begin at eight a.m. He would have missed them. Likely, he is still in transit or has just arrived. All this assumes he was flying commercial."

Aubrey rubbed his eyes. Transatlantic flights always muddled his thinking. "So, there *is at least* another guy connected to this," he said. "He's got Mom hidden away somewhere. We've got to get to her before Duric does." Remembrance of all the ways his uncle had killed people sent cortisol rushing through his body with "fight" signals. But there was no one to fight.

"None of us is safe," said Aubrey. "We need to relocate before he gets back to Chicago. Dad grab some gear."

CHAPTER THIRTEEN

Stana's kidnapping shook Meredith to the core. But she had to go on air tonight. She couldn't do anything for Stana at this point, but she could at least make certain her own mother was safe.

She put in a call.

"Hi, Mom," she said. "Just calling to tell you we're back from Bosnia."

"I'm glad," her mother said. "I didn't tell you, because it was silly, of course, but I was afraid you were going to get blown up."

"Uh, you might want to take a little trip to the cabin."

"Why on earth?"

"My colleague that I traveled with? His mom was just kidnapped. It's a long tale, and I don't have time to tell you everything now. I'm going to be on air tonight with the story. You might want to watch the ten o'clock news." Her mother had WOOT on cable. "I wouldn't want anything to happen to you. Just to set my mind at rest, could you go?"

"Oh, honey, that's awful news. Are you in danger?"

"I'm relying on the FBI. They're setting up a safe house for us. Please make an airline reservation and if you can't fly out tonight, spend the night in a hotel."

"I will, but you've got to promise you'll keep in touch, sweetie. I'm going to be worried sick."

Meredith drew a steadying breath. "I have a new cell number, so be sure to check this call on your phone."

"Of course, I'll worry. I'm your mom."

"I love you," Meredith said. "Please just go get packed."

* * *

Just before she was to go on air, Aubrey called.

"We have the safe house all lined up. Agent Marks will be there to pick you up after your broadcast. We don't want you driving out here in your car because someone could be watching the station. We've figured out Duric didn't kidnap my mother. He couldn't have gotten here in time."

Meredith's scalp prickled. "So, someone else is involved?"

"Yes. And that someone or those someones could be following you."

"All right. Okay, so, I've got to go."

"Knock their socks off."

"Bye."

Meredith's mouth was uncharacteristically dry as she gave her newscast, fashioning it to fit the new facts which had come to light only that day.

> *In breaking news tonight, Mrs. Stana Kettering [visual] has been kidnapped from her home in Hyde Park. The family and the FBI believe the abduction is the work of Zoran Duric, [visual] a Bosnian war criminal. He is considered to be extremely dangerous and will not hesitate to take lives if he is confronted. It is not known if he speaks English.*
>
> *Mrs. Kettering's husband, Dr. William Kettering is a professor of Balkan history and politics at the University of Chicago. He is offering a reward for any information which may lead to the recovery of his wife.*
>
> *Zoran Duric is currently being investigated by the FBI in connection with crimes of genocide committed in Bosnia during the war in 1992–1995. He has also committed recent crimes against our journalists. A more detailed story on Duric will appear in a later broadcast.*
>
> *Do not attempt to confront this man. If you know anything which may be pertinent to this investigation you are urged to contact the FBI.*
>
> *Duric's crimes were especially heinous and were committed primarily against the Bosnian Muslims, or Bosniak's, whom he blames for the death of his son. Zoran Duric was a major aggressor in the massacre which took place in Zvornik along the border with Serbia in 1992. We will be doing future newscasts on this man, what motivated him, and what crimes he is still committing in Bosnia.*
>
> *[Picture of Doric shown again] If anyone sees this fugitive, we would urge you to contact either our WOOT tip line [phone number displayed] or the FBI [phone number displayed].*

After her story, one of her fellow journalists was shown interviewing the alarmed Imam at the Cultural Center.

Mr. Q congratulated her on her broadcast. "That was stellar. Especially after the day you've had. That Marks fellow from the FBI is waiting for you in my office. Keep in touch."

"We'll give you the story as it unfolds," she promised.

* * *

On the way to the safe house, Agent Marks asked her, "Did you make any attempt to notify local law enforcement in Sarajevo about those attempts on your life?"

"We did after the bombing. We spoke with Major General Waldner, the head of EUFOR in Bosnia, and briefed him about Duric. They had soldiers escorting and guarding us from then until we left."

"Have they had any success at all, do you know?"

"They're doing their best to bring him in, but so far they say he's too quick for them. Always a jump ahead," said Meredith. She told him the story of Ibrisimovic and his brother.

"Sounds like one bad human," said Marks. "I'll get in touch with our DC office and have them coordinate with EUFOR."

"The man's a catalyst for war and disruption," said Meredith. "We're afraid he's going to do something really awful and shatter the peace accords." She sighed heavily, suddenly exhausted. She gave him an account of the drive-by shooting. "Fortunately, again, we weren't hurt, but others were. We escaped and, thanks to EUFOR, were out of the country within the hour."

"This definitely isn't a person we want loose in Chicago," said Marks. "By the way, we have a couple of other agents at the safe house. We can't be too careful."

"Has the kidnapper made any demands?"

"At the time I left to pick you up, he hadn't. But, then Dr. Kettering doesn't have a cell phone. Since this was the work of a confederate, we are back to square one. We have no prospects."

"Well," said Meredith, "All WOOT's viewers have seen the photo of Duric. We should get some tips on our hotline from people who have seen him. He's quite distinctive looking."

"It's always good to have the press on your side," said Agent Marks. "Aubrey said you have interviews with a number of people in Sarajevo who witnessed his crimes."

"Yes. When we get to the house, I'll give you the jump drive from my computer. You'll need a translator. Both Professor Kettering and Aubrey speak Serbo-Croatian."

"This isn't the time for them to be buried in Duric's war crimes. We'll send it to Washington for translation. They can make us a transcript."

Meredith took to the safe house immediately. It was in Glen Ellyn, one of her favorite suburbs. It had a stone and stucco exterior, a strong, steel-reinforced oak front door, and plantation shutters which gave them plenty of privacy. The walls were painted a rich latte color, and there were three bedrooms which accommodated them adequately.

She went immediately to Aubrey and caught one of his hands in hers. "I can't even imagine how your mother is coping."

"I take a bit of comfort in the fact that she is a survivor," said Dr. Kettering. "You wouldn't believe what she went through during the war. Also, Duric is her brother. She knows him well."

"It's late," said Aubrey. "You've had the ultimate long day. I think you need to get to bed."

"What are you going to do?" Meredith asked.

"I have no idea. But I know I can't sleep," Aubrey said.

Without a word, Meredith headed for the kitchen where she intended to make both Aubrey and her one of his mother's special drinks. Fortunately, the safe house had milk and honey. Nutmeg was too much to hope for.

"Does this place have a den or something, where we can curl up in front of a fireplace?"

"It does," Aubrey said.

A few minutes later, drinks in hand, they went into a small, cozy room with brown corduroy couches. Aubrey turned on the gas fire.

"We need to chronicle everything we know about Duric for the FBI," Aubrey said.

"We can do that when we're more rested. My brain is fried, and you are hopped up on adrenaline."

Aubrey began to pace. "This is all my fault. I never should have brought my parents into this."

"There is no way you could have known that Duric was your mother's brother. If it's anyone's fault, it's mine. I was way too anxious to get this story. I had no idea it would have personal repercussions."

"I should have followed my father's advice and left Duric alone," Aubrey said. "I will never forgive myself if something happens to my mother."

"Come here, Aubrey," she said. "Sit down on this couch." She patted the back of the couch in front of her.

Still absorbed in his self-flagellation, he took a seat. Placing her hands on his shoulders, she began massaging the knotted muscles.

Conversation halted as she worked. It was a tough job. Aubrey was very, very tense.

"Don't fall into a pit of self-blame," she said finally, her voice soft. "We need your brilliance to stop this guy."

He said nothing.

Finally, asleep on her feet, she said, "I have to get some sleep, or I'll be no good tomorrow." She kissed the top of his head. "Good night, Aubrey."

"Thanks, Meredith," he said, his voice low. "Good night."

* * *

The next morning, she found Aubrey asleep on the couch where she had left him. His father was in the kitchen sitting over a cup of coffee, talking to the FBI agents.

She had an idea first thing this morning. "I wonder if Father Savic down at the church in Lansing knows your wife is missing," she said to Aubrey's father. "He might be able to help us get the word out in the Serbian community. Duric could have some confederates Father Savic might know about."

Dr. Kettering pounced on this idea. "Aubrey mentioned that. That's something I can look into. I'll call him right now. I know the man well."

"Good idea," said Agent Marks. "We've been wondering where to turn next. The FBI tip line got some calls after your broadcast, but they've been working on them all night, and nothing has panned out."

Meredith set up her computer on the kitchen table. "I'm going to write an account of everything that happened before we went to Bosnia. I think best when I am writing. Maybe something will come to me." She fired up the computer. There was an open document. "Hold on. It looks like Aubrey was already ahead of me. There are pages of notes here you need to see."

Dr. Kettering reentered the room.

"Father Savic is going to meet us at FBI headquarters and brainstorm with us. I didn't think he should come here. He is seriously worried. He says he may have some ideas. I'll wake Aubrey."

Meredith thought they all probably needed fuel other than coffee. She found some cold cereal and set about cutting up fresh melon and bananas.

Aubrey stumbled into the room and poured himself some coffee.

"Here," Meredith said. "You've got to eat something."

* * *

Father Savic was waiting for them when they arrived at headquarters. The cleric was dressed in his robes and seemed a bit out of place in the modern FBI building.

"Father Savic, thank you so much for coming," said Dr. Kettering, rising to meet him as he entered the conference room.

"I would do anything for my Stana. She is one of the lights of my life," the priest said. "What do you need from me?"

Aubrey said, "Zoran Doric hates my mother for what he sees as a betrayal when she married my father and came to this country."

Dr. Kettering said, "He hates the Americans almost as much as he hates the Muslims."

"We've been in Sarajevo, and he followed us there," said Meredith. "The problem with our theory that Doric is the kidnapper is that he couldn't have returned here in enough time to have accomplished it."

Aubrey pulled out his phone and showed the recent picture of the terrorist they had obtained in Sarajevo. "EUFOR got this picture of him."

Agent Marks said, "We're thinking now that he must have a confederate somewhere."

Father Savic nodded.

"We're wondering if his confederate is someone he knew from the old days," said Meredith. "Have you ever heard of any Bosnian Serb war criminals who came here after the war?"

"As a matter of fact, I have been thinking about that," said Savic. "There *was* someone. I never met him, so I don't remember his name. But there was a furor among the men of the Serb National Federation, our benevolent society. Some of them wanted to turn him in, some of them didn't. Both sides were emphatic."

Though the news was what they needed, Meredith rubbed her arms with her hands. She had difficulty getting her mind around the fact that there was more than one lunatic out there.

"How did they resolve the issue?" asked Aubrey.

"He was not admitted to the local lodge of the Federation; I know that. But the matter just seemed to disappear after a few months. I'm guessing that the man got out of the neighborhood and changed his name."

"Thank you, Father," said Aubrey. "This is a good lead. I didn't even think about the Federation. Is there a lodge in Lansing?"

"Yes. As a matter of fact, we're holding our fall bowling tournament tomorrow."

Aubrey put his hands in his pockets, and for the first time since he had found his mother was missing, she saw a gleam in his eye.

"You're going to go undercover," she guessed.

"I sure am," he replied. He asked the cleric, "How do I sign up?"

"Everything is done online these days. I imagine that would be the fastest way. But you'll have to buy an insurance policy from them as part of the deal."

"Awesome," he said. "I'm going to need an alias. What is a good Serbian name that wouldn't make me stick out? Sort of like the equivalent of Jones or Smith?"

"You can't lose with a name like Anton Popovic," said the priest with a smile.

"This is a real long shot," objected Dr. Kettering, a deep frown creasing his forehead.

"Do you have a better idea?" asked Aubrey.

"I'll think of one, I'm sure," his father said.

"Well, while you're thinking, I'm acting." Aubrey began scrolling through his phone.

"I can call my friend, Allie, and see if her father knows anything about the war criminal," said Meredith. "He might have heard something."

"Who is her father?" asked the priest.

"Mikal Novak. He's a Croatian recluse. Bosnian Serbs killed his wife in the war."

"That's a good idea," said Agent Marks.

Though they questioned the priest for another half hour, no further leads developed.

Meredith turned to Father Savic and thanked him for coming and helping them.

"Stay in touch," the priest said. "I will be praying for you, as will the rest of my congregation. Stana is well-loved."

Dr. Kettering shook his hand and clapped him on the back. "Thank you for coming, Father."

"I need to call Allie," Meredith said. She tried, but the phone went to voicemail. "She must be talking to someone. Remind me to call her later, Aubrey."

CHAPTER FOURTEEN

When they returned to the safe house, Aubrey suggested that he and Meredith go into the den. He was at loose ends and didn't want to irritate his father with his own anxiety. His dad had enough to deal with.

"I haven't had a chance to tell you, but I don't have a good feeling about your going bowling with the Serbs tomorrow," Meredith said.

"Look, Meredith. Compared to what we've just been through, bowling with a bunch of Serbian-Americans is a walk in the park. What's the problem?"

She looked down at her lap. "I'm sorry. I know you feel like you need to do something. It's just that we've always been together before."

"You think I can't handle things myself?" He felt a spur of irritation but quelled it. Meredith had been through a lot.

"Forgive me. This isn't really about you. It's about me. I'm worried about you." Looking into her eyes, he realized she was more than serious. She was scared. Was he flattering himself or did this have something to do with her fiancé's horrible death?

He put a hand on her arm. "How about if I take my Glock? I'll even wear it on my hip so everyone can see it."

She attempted a smile but couldn't seem to pull it off. "They'll think you're a seriously bad dude. It might be kind of hard to ask casual questions if you have a gun."

"You're right. I'll have to conceal it in my waistband under my bowling shirt. I'm not a bad bowler, by the way."

"That doesn't surprise me," she said. "You're a man of many talents. Some of them are even useful."

They sipped coffee and gazed into the fire. Though he was trying hard to act normally, he was sick with worry about his mother in the hands of someone like Duric. And who knew what his confederate was like? He looked at the woman beside him. She had her own worries, her own nightmares. He hated to pull her into his. Especially after all she had been through with him in Bosnia.

"Do you feel like you could talk to me about Jan, Meredith? I think that's what this is really about."

Turning her face away, she appeared to study the gas log fire.

He sensed her closing off from him, but he was determined to draw her out. "Was he in the Middle East on a service mission?"

"No. He was a journalist like me. We worked together in Africa before that."

"Whose idea was it to visit the Christian refugee camp?"

"His."

"And I take it he was a dedicated Christian."

"So am I, as a matter of fact," Meredith said.

"Oh."

She said, "They could just as easily have taken me." Her voice was soft, and he was afraid she was going to start to cry. Something in him urged him to press on with his questions.

"Tell me about him. What was he like?"

"He was an idealist." She spoke slowly, as though she were a great distance off. "Jan wanted to put the world right. He was funny and smart and capable of immense devotion. It was a sort of overwhelming thing to be the subject of that kind of devotion."

Jan was obviously her hero. Aubrey didn't feel terribly heroic himself and suddenly sensed that he would never be more than a side act in her life. He continued with his questions, eager to know more about the man the memory of whom he was pitted against.

"I imagine it was. What kind of family did he come from?"

Her eyes were huge with sadness as she turned to face him. "It was pretty dysfunctional. He was the oldest. His mother was a perpetual invalid in a wheelchair. His father drank. They fought."

"That stinks," he said. Maybe stirring up these memories was cruel rather than helpful. Leaning forward with his elbows on his knees, he tried to think of something else to say. Finally, he said, "You must have had all kinds of wonderful plans for your own family."

"We did. We talked about it a lot." Her voice broke on the words.

Acting on instinct, he pulled her to him. "Come here," he said. He patted her back while she wept. "Life is rotten sometimes."

"Like when your mom gets kidnapped," she said in a croaky little voice. "You should be crying on my shoulder, not vice versa."

"I shouldn't have brought up such a painful subject," he said.

"How are *you* handling things?" she asked, staying wrapped in his arms but now searching his eyes.

"I'm angry. And scared for my mom. You know what kind of man Duric is."

"Tell me about your mom. She seems like a unique person."

Holding her head on his chest, he began to speak. "She was a wonderful mother in spite of her challenges with anxiety and PTSD. She was so determined to learn English! She could speak her own language with Dad and her friends, but she learned English for me. She wanted to be able to be part of my life at school and with my friends."

"And she taught you Serbo-Croatian?"

"I sort of just picked it up. It was the language we spoke at home when I was really young. After a while, she insisted we speak English.

"She read to me. Even when I was older, we read Tolkien's *Lord of the Rings* together. That was an adventure. We sat up late, drinking cocoa. She made quilts, and we always had one or two wrapped around us in the winter when she read."

"It sounds idyllic," Meredith said.

"Until the war came, my mother did have an idyllic life with her parents. She told me stories. I wish I could have known them." He brooded.

He went on. "Winter always reminds me of my mother. We ice skated together, and she taught me to bake. I owe my interest in cooking to her. It was something we could do together.

"She came to all my hockey games. In the spring we planted her garden together, but I always disappeared conveniently when it was time to weed in the summer."

He paused, his throat suddenly tight. "I always knew she was fragile. My father treats her like a piece of china. This is so awful because he always tried to shelter her as much as he could from unhappiness.

"But Mom doesn't hide from life. She takes it on. She was determined to assimilate and become a true American."

"What a mother you have! She sounds like the kind of person who is tougher than you think."

They sat looking into the fire. Finally, he said, "I sure hope so."

"I don't know why, but I keep getting the feeling that I need to call Allie. Like she might know something for some reason."

Taking her phone out of her purse, she tried again to call her friend as Aubrey watched.

"Voicemail again," she said.

* * *

That afternoon, Meredith received a phone call from Mr. Q. He asked if she would be available to come down to the station for a follow-up interview for the news that night. They were interviewing Serbian-Americans from the Federation and Father Savic about their thoughts regarding Zoran Duric and his terror tactics. They had also found friends of Stana's in Father Savic's congregation to talk about her.

"To show what a desperate character this Duric is, we want a first-hand account of the bombing and the drive-by shooting you were involved in."

She put him on hold while she consulted with Agent Marks.

"I suppose that would be all right if we accompany you. Agents Murphy and Casson could remain here," the agent said.

She told Mr. Q they would leave for the station shortly.

"Better you than me," Aubrey said. "Do you want me to come with you?"

"I think you need to stay here with your dad."

* * *

The interview was difficult. It was much different to be the interviewee rather than the interviewer. At the end of Meredith's account of the two attacks, the interviewer, a colleague of hers named Brooke Hansen, asked, "How have these experiences impacted you personally?"

"I am dismayed," Meredith said. "The war happened when I was a baby, yet for this man, Zoran Duric, it is still going on. I am very anxious for him and the men working with him to be apprehended before they can commit acts which could spark another war.

"Also, I would like to say that this man does not represent all Serbs. Stana Kettering and her friends, not to mention some wonderful people we met in Bosnia are very open and loving people. They want to put old hatreds behind them. I would ask that you viewers help them to do this by aiding in the capture of Zoran Duric and whatever confederates he may have working with him."

When it was done, Meredith felt as limp as a wet dishrag. She said little to the agents as they drove back to Glen Ellyn.

They found Aubrey and his dad eating pizza for dinner with Agents Murphy and Casson. Though Meredith wasn't hungry, she made a salad and insisted that everyone share it. Soon it was time for the six o'clock news.

The story was again the main headline. Meredith's entire interview was aired, along with Father Savic's, and one of Stana's friends. Again, the telephone tip lines were shown.

"You did very well, honey," said Aubrey.

Dr. Kettering agreed. "I appreciate your mention of 'good Serbs.' I'm afraid all this publicity may aggravate old prejudices."

Agent Marks spoke to Aubrey. "I want an agent with you when you leave tomorrow. Not only for your safety but because if he wants to kill you, that may draw him out. It may be the best way to catch him."

Meredith buried her face in her hands. "I wish I'd never gotten that horrible anonymous phone call. I don't want you to get killed!"

He put a comforting arm around her shoulders and pulled her to his side. "I'm not going to get killed, and you're going to get your story—the exposé of a sociopath."

"I don't care about the story anymore," she said. "All I want is you and your mother safe."

His father echoed her, "This is nasty, Aubrey."

"And I'm pretty sure he has help," said Aubrey. "And that kidnapping my mother and killing me is not his endgame. I've got to try to find his confederate. This jaunt tomorrow isn't because I just want something to do."

Meredith straightened. "We'll figure it out," she said.

No one got much sleep that night. Aubrey fixed a huge breakfast for everyone at five a.m. There were pancakes, eggs, bacon, orange juice, even grits.

"Whoever heard of a safe house with grits?" he asked.

After breakfast he took a long, hot shower. He would stop at his mother's church to pick up some "immigrant clothes," from the charity bin, but in the meantime he dressed in a t-shirt and jeans.

* * *

Their nighttime agents had left, and Special Agents Marks and Steele were at the house when Aubrey came back downstairs. They had brought another agent with them and introduced him as Agent McGuire who was short and well-muscled with a buzz cut. He was dressed in jeans and a White Sox t-shirt to accompany Aubrey on his sortie to the bowling alley in Lansing.

"I know how to be unobtrusive," the man insisted.

Aubrey was not pleased, but for his father's and Meredith's sake, he went along with the plan. Before he left, he took Meredith with him back into the den and closed the door.

"I'm going to be fine," he said. "And hopefully I'm going to pick up some information that will help me find my mother. Why don't you try calling your friend again while I'm gone and work on the presentation of your exposé?"

She ignored his words, fixing her eyes on his.

"Kiss me," she said.

"Really?" he asked.

"Really. For luck, or whatever. Just kiss me, Aubrey."

The kiss was long, slow, and deep. She tasted like mint toothpaste, and it still stirred him to his core. Holding her to his chest when they had finished, he felt her melt against him as she said, "Wow. Just wow."

"I agree. Wow."

With obvious reluctance, she pulled away. "If you find out anything about a possible confederate, don't run off half-cocked, Aubrey."

"I can't. Agent McGuire will see to that."

CHAPTER FIFTEEN

Meredith's heart throbbed in her throat as she watched Aubrey and Agent McGuire drive away in their unobtrusive Honda Accord. That kiss. Wow again. She had felt their connection clear through her. Jan had never kissed her like that. Or if he had, she had never responded like that.

She felt suddenly guilty as though she were a widow or something. Didn't she owe more to Jan's memory?

And now, she was worried all out of proportion. What could happen to Aubrey when he was with an FBI minder, anyway?

Sighing, she decided she would call Allie to take her mind off her fears. Again, the phone went to voicemail.

Frustrated and a little uneasy, she tried calling her friend's clinic. Allie's receptionist answered.

"Novak Veterinary Clinic, this is Megan speaking."

"Megan, this is Meredith Montgomery. I'm looking for Allie. Is she there this morning?"

"Oh, Meredith! I'm so glad you called. I'm really worried about Allie. She seems to have disappeared. I haven't seen her since the day before yesterday."

Meredith couldn't take it in. "Disappeared? Allie? She hasn't called in or anything?"

"No. And her cell seems to be turned off."

"Have you been to her condo?"

"No. I don't have keys or anything."

"I'll see what I can do, Megan. Don't worry. Just hold the fort at the clinic. That's what Allie would expect you to do."

"If you find out anything, would you let me know? Should I call the police?"

"I'll take care of it, Megan."

"Agent Marks, I have a situation. I don't think it's connected to our case, but it's something I need to follow up on."

He tilted his head to the side.

She sat on the couch, and he chose the club chair. Agent Steele was still in the kitchen speaking with the professor.

"I have a friend who's missing. She's disappeared. She's my closest friend. I need to have someone check on her."

"And there is no way this could be connected to our case? What about someone trying to manipulate you by holding her hostage?"

"I suppose that's possible, but I don't even know how they could have found out about our friendship. Could you call in Allie's disappearance and have someone check her condo? She lives at 545 Hinman in Evanston. Top floor. She's a vet and has her own clinic, but she never showed up yesterday, and her receptionist says Allie has had her phone turned off since then. By the way, she's the daughter of a Bosnian-Croatian, not that that means anything."

"Well, since it looks like it would be a case for us even if it isn't connected, I'll call it in and have someone check it out. Does she have a boyfriend?"

"No. And she's not the type to get picked up by a guy. She doesn't do that scene."

"Okay. Anything else I should know? Where does her father live?"

"Lake Forest. You know, I think I should go in with your agents. I know what to look for."

"Let's wait on this until we have the police do a check of the condo. Kidnapping is our bailiwick, but maybe they can save you some unnecessary grief if they find all is well."

With bad grace, Meredith agreed, though she wanted to leave right away.

"What kind of car does she drive?"

"A baby blue VW beetle."

Agent Steele made the call to the Evanston police, who agreed to send someone in to check the condo.

It was an hour before the agent received their report. Her face looked grave as she disconnected the call.

"They found the door open, not locked. There was no sign of Ms. Novak. The back door had been jimmied. Her car sat in front of the condo."

Meredith set her jaw. She was going to find Allie.

* * *

While the two new agents, Jackson and Casson, who were assigned to this new case drove her to Allie's condo, Meredith did her best to explain her worry about Allie.

"So, this guy who kidnapped Mrs. Kettering is a whack job, and you think he might have kidnapped your best friend?" asked Agent Casson, a blond-haired Chris Pine clone. His partner was a towering African American.

"Why?" asked Jackson.

"It doesn't make sense, and I don't know why. I haven't even talked to Allie lately. I've been out of the country."

The condo occupied the third floor of a brick building with a center courtyard. Meredith swayed a bit while climbing the stairs as her almost sleepless night caught up with her.

She knocked on the door of the condo, though she didn't expect anyone to answer. A policeman answered. The agents introduced themselves and Meredith.

"Thanks for keeping an eye on things," Agent Jackson said.

The police officer, a brunette woman, said, "We already talked to the neighbors no one heard anything."

Meredith asked, "May I come in now?"

The police officer held out gloves and shoe coverings. "Put these on first."

Jackson told her, "Let me photograph the place as it is before you touch anything."

Her friend had excellent taste but was no housekeeper. Her untidiness always made Meredith itch to put things in order. The rooms were all painted stark white, and the floors had a natural oak finish. Allie had chosen a Scandinavian look, so the rooms sported bright blue, red, and yellow accents over white and gray furniture. Magazines and books lay in piles everywhere—mostly having to do with her profession.

"Phone in here!" Casson shouted from the kitchen. "Looks like she was making dinner. The whole place smells like onions."

Meredith walked through the dining room to the kitchen. "She would never have left her phone!" she said. "Look! She was wearing her earbuds. She liked opera. She wouldn't have heard a thing."

Translucent onions congealed in a frying pan. A package of ground beef spoiled on the counter next to the stove. Cans of tomato sauce sat unopened.

"She was making her spaghetti sauce."

"Yeah," said Casson. "I've got the room photographed. Someone forced the back door."

Meredith noted the splintered door at the end of the kitchen. "There are black marks on the floor like she was dragged," she said. "She wore black Nikes to work."

"She was taken, looks like." He frowned. "Sorry, ma'am. I know she was your friend."

Though she had more than half expected it, the reality engulfed her in fresh fear. Who in the world would kidnap Allie? She tried to swallow the lump in her throat and tears stung her eyes.

"I'm going to look in her home office and see if I can find anything that might explain this."

When she went back to the other end of the condo, she found Agent Jackson had just finished photographing the oak-paneled room.

"I hate this," she said. "I feel like I'm invading her privacy."

"Goes with the territory," said Agent Jackson.

Meredith looked through the desk. Allie was a coupon hoarder. A file of coupons filled one whole drawer. Office supplies crowded together in the next drawer. The middle drawer had photo prints of trips she had taken to the Grand Canyon, the Cayman Islands, and New York. Meredith swallowed the lump again. A tear fell.

They had gone to New York together to see the shows. It had been a great week.

She went over to the file cabinet. Tax documents for the last five years. Drafts of articles she'd written for Vet journals.

The bottom drawer was a surprise.

Allie is a closet romance writer.

At least a half-dozen drafts of what looked like an Amish romance set in a dystopian future crowded the space of the drawer, bursting out of files: *Research, World-Building, Character sketches, Drafts.*

She felt like a voyeur. If Allie had wanted her to know about this hobby, she would have told her.

Meredith stood up. "There's nothing here that sheds any light on things. And other than the fact that she was born in Bosnia, there is really no connection to this case."

"Wait," said Casson. "Are you talking about the kidnapping of the Bosnian Kettering woman?"

"Yeah. But that man's of Serbian descent. Allie's people were Croatian. Water and oil. And she didn't know anything about the case, anyway. She wasn't the least interested in the war."

"But what about her parents?"

"Her mother was killed by Serbs in the war. Her father lives in seclusion somewhere on the North Shore. He's never even talked to Allie about the war. It makes him sad."

"I found something odd," Agent Jackson called from the bedroom. "In her sweater drawer. A letter. Handwritten. 'To be opened upon my death.' It's even sealed with sealing wax."

Meredith hurried into the bedroom and looked at the find in the agent's gloved hands. "That's not Allie's writing. Her handwriting is very distinctive—a combination of printing and cursive. And she always uses a broad point Sharpie."

The agent slid it into an evidence bag. "We'll have them take a look at it in the lab. Fingerprints. Handwriting analysis."

"You're going to open it?" Meredith asked.

"Part of our job. It is probably from her father. Could be the link you're looking for."

"You're right, of course."

Curiosity and impatience gnawed at her. She wondered if the letter held answers.

"Can we go to the lab now?" she asked.

"We need to get you back to the safe house. Then, we'll take it in. We'll call you as soon as we read it."

"If I were Allie, I would have opened that long ago!" she said, with a flash of annoyance at her friend.

"Maybe she was afraid of the contents," said Agent Jackson. "Maybe she didn't want to know what it said."

The agents took apart the furniture, looked on the underside of drawers and even went through the freezer. They found nothing else of interest.

Trying to force the image of Allie being pulled from the apartment out of her mind, she agreed it was time to leave.

Where was Allie? Was she hurt? In spite of the absurdity of the idea, did this have anything to do with Bosnia and Duric?

As soon as she was in the Honda sedan, she took out her hand sanitizer and scrubbed her hands over and over.

"Will you notify her father?"

"Do you have a name for us?"

"All I know him by is Mr. Novak. He lives in Lake Forest. I met him once years ago."

"We'll take care of it," said Agent Casson.

"Thanks."

CHAPTER SIXTEEN

Dressed in worn, out of style jeans and a faded work shirt, Aubrey joined the Serbian Federation's bowling team at Bowl-a-Thon in downtown Lansing. He was greeted enthusiastically in Serbo-Croatian.

"Welcome! You must be Anton Popovic," said a long, lean man with shaggy hair and a big smile who looked to be in his fifties. "We're glad you could join us today! Where are you from?"

Aubrey had his alias carefully prepared. "In the Republika Srpska--Zvornik."

"I'm Bosko, and this fellow," he indicated a husky twenty-something, "Is Milovoj."

He introduced five or six others, but Aubrey knew their names would go right out of his head. He concentrated on remembering Bosko and Milovoj.

The bowling alley smelled of floor polish, old shoes, and ancient cigarette smoke. Some of the ceiling lights were out.

Aubrey rented a pair of shoes and a bowling ball and went to the lane where the Serbian guys were gathered, exchanging insults and taunts about each other's bowling skills. They appeared to be of all ages.

Even though there were several men Bosko's age, everyone appeared boisterous and happy to be spending the day together.

"We play three frames, then have lunch," said Bosko.

The first game got underway. Fortunately, he had grown up bowling with his mother in the neighborhood family league, but it had been years since he'd lifted a bowling ball.

"I'm a bit rusty," he said. "I haven't done this too often."

"Well, we're glad you joined us," said Milovoj. "I'm the one you bought your insurance from."

"Ah," said Aubrey with a laugh. Buying insurance had been a weird pre-requisite for joining the Federation.

The games were actually fun, and he relaxed, enjoying the company of these men who mostly held jobs in the steel mills during the week. They were all fairly new to America, which was why they still spoke their mother tongue. During the games, he found out that most of them or their families had come since the war. This fact made them perfect for Aubrey's purposes.

His FBI minder, Agent McGuire, sat in the coffee shop watching. Aubrey, feeling himself in no danger, actually forgot he was even there.

When lunchtime came, Bosko seated himself next to Aubrey in the coffee shop. They both ordered chili dogs and fries.

"So, you were probably too young to remember the war in Zvornik," Bosko said. Aubrey was surprised that his new friend brought up the subject.

"I was about five," he said. "I remember lots of screaming and shooting. I remember the smell of the cellar of my house where my mama and papa used to take me until they were killed."

"I was in Zvornik, as well. Though I am Serbian, I do not hesitate to say it was a bloodbath. I am sorry your parents were killed."

"My grandmother tells me it was an accident. They were in the wrong place at the wrong time."

"I do not mean to wound you, but she was probably sparing your feelings. A lot of Serbs died in the fighting. It was brutal. People were crazy with bloodlust."

"It still goes on, you know," said Aubrey. "The killing."

"Is that why you came to this country?" asked Bosko, his eyes curious and something else Aubrey could not read. He grew uneasy.

"Yes. My grandmother and I saved our money for a long time so that I could have this opportunity."

Bosko looked around him, as though checking for eavesdroppers. "Do you speak English?"

"No," said Aubrey, knowing he could never fake an accent. "Why?"

"No worries. I have just heard some rumors lately that trouble me. I am not sure who is to be trusted."

"Rumors?"

"Have you heard the name Zoran Duric?"

Aubrey had a hard time maintaining his composure. "My grandmother spoke of him. She said he was evil. She never said so explicitly, but I got the idea that he was responsible for the 'accident' that caused my parents' death."

"He is here. He has been seen. Father Savic told me."

"That is bad. But this is not Zvornik. What can he do?"

"Muslims are pouring into Chicago," said Bosko. "If he does anything to carry out his vendetta against them, it will be bad for all Serbs. The media will bring up Zvornik and all the other battles of ethnic cleansing."

"Have you heard of any specific plans?" Aubrey asked hesitantly. "Maybe you could go to the FBI."

"No. I haven't heard of any plans. But you know the FBI better than I do. I saw that man over there." He indicated Agent McGuire. "He doesn't bowl. He just drinks coffee and watches you."

Aubrey's heart began to pound and his palms to sweat. Whose side was Bosko on? He decided to go for broke. Without acknowledging the truthfulness of the man's guess, he asked, "Were there many war criminals that came to Chicago after the war? Maybe Duric has some confederates here."

"Ah! That is what you want to know. There was one—Drasko Subotic—but he was ostracized in our community. You must understand, we did not want to be associated with what the Bosnian Serbs did in the war. There was a stigma. I think Subotic went to another city, or maybe somewhere in Europe. He was never tried in the Hague."

"You have never seen him since?"

"No. It is possible he took on another identity, I suppose. Where did you learn to speak such fine Serbo-Croatian?" he asked in English.

"My mother," Aubrey answered easily. "I am not from Zvornik, but Votopad. My parents were not killed in the war. If you go to Father Savic's church, you know my mother. She is Stana Kettering." He forbore giving the man her maiden name, as his mother guarded the secret fiercely. "She has been kidnapped by a confederate of Duric's we believe. That is why I'm trying to find him."

Bosko emitted a Bosnian curse. "You are trying to find her, find Duric. You think he stays with a confederate. That is the purpose for your charade today. Well, you will not find him among these people. I know them."

Aubrey took out his phone. "I hope you'll forgive my deception. Let's exchange phone numbers, in case you hear anything else. Any other rumors."

They gave each other their numbers, and then Aubrey stood up and shook hands with Bosko. "I haven't bowled in years. It was fun. Thanks."

He walked out of the bowling alley with McGuire joining him in a few minutes at the car.

"I was made," Aubrey told the agent.

McGuire said, "I saw you talking to him pretty earnestly. Did he have anything for us?"

He told the agent all about their conversation. "I probably didn't deserve to succeed in my clever plan, but it worked anyway. There was one war criminal that appeared here and then disappeared when he was ostracized. His name was Drasko Subotic. Could you run that through whatever databases you have at the bureau and see if we can come up with a photograph, maybe even an address?"

"Will do. Good work, even if I blew it for you. Of course, there is no way of knowing if this is the one working with Duric."

"No. But at least it's a start."

* * *

When they arrived at the safe house, he found Meredith nervously scrubbing the kitchen floor on her hands and knees.

"Oh, Aubrey!" She stood up. "I'm so glad you're safe! Did you find out anything?"

"Some agent I make! The guy practically fed me my lines. I was made."

He told her what had happened.

"Drasko Subotic," she repeated. Then, "I have some awful news. Allie has been kidnapped, too."

He listened in shock as she outlined her call to the clinic and their visit to Allie's condo.

"So, I'm waiting to hear what the letter says," she concluded. "The FBI is notifying her father."

"Do you think Allie fits into our story?"

"I don't know. There's only the Bosnian War connection. And Mr. Novak and Zoran Duric fought on different sides. But I am anxious to hear what the letter says. Maybe it will shed some light. I wish I'd hear from them."

Meredith went back to her scrubbing.

CHAPTER SEVENTEEN

When Agents Casson and Jackson came to relieve Agents Marks and Steele for the night, they brought a copy of the letter to Allie from her father. They said they had no news on the kidnapping. They also told Aubrey that there was nothing in the FBI database on Drasko Subotic.

Meredith eagerly read the copy of the letter. Dr. Kettering and Aubrey read over her shoulder.

My dear daughter,

I just want to let you know that no matter what you may hear about me now that I am gone, I have always loved you. War brings out a terrible side of men. I did things I am not proud of in that life. But I have always been proud of you.

I am enclosing a receipt and a key for a safety deposit box in downtown Chicago. You will find that in it I have some mementos of the war. They are quite valuable. What you do with them is up to you. I admit I did not come by them honestly.

I love you, and I loved your mother,

Dad

Meredith was disappointed. But Aubrey seized on it. "He was a war criminal! A Croatian war criminal!"

"Do you think the stuff in the safety deposit box is war loot?" she asked.

"Without a doubt," Aubrey said.

"No wonder he didn't like talking about the war," said Dr. Kettering.

"He's been in hiding all these years. Of course, Novak isn't his real name," said Aubrey.

The two FBI agents were sitting at the end of the table, eating pizza.

"You didn't see any photos of her father while you were looking through her condo, did you?" asked Agent Jackson.

Photos!

"Yes," said Meredith. "There were photos. But I don't remember if there were pictures of her father. There could have been. They were photos of vacations." She put her hands on her hips. "Now I need to look at them again. Which one of you is going to take me back over there?" she asked the agents.

"I'll take you," said Agent Jackson, getting up from the table. "Do you need something to eat, first?"

"I can't eat. This is too important. I'll bet you anything there is a photo there!"

"I'm coming, too," said Aubrey.

"No," said Meredith. "Let's not duplicate efforts. It would be better if you stay here and research Subotic in the *Trib.* My little mission may come to nothing, and we need to find out who this guy is."

* * *

Once again, the door to Allie's apartment was open. The police seal was broken, and tape hung all around the door. Agent Jackson put a finger to his lips signaling silence and walked in ahead of her, Glock at the ready.

She watched from the living room as he went back to the kitchen, his arm fully extended, holding his weapon in front of him.

Suddenly a shape came barreling out of Allie's office in the other direction. He ran into Meredith in the doorway and knocked her down. With a ski mask over his face, he was unrecognizable as he pulled her to her feet.

He made a sound of satisfaction, just as Jackson appeared in the doorway of the kitchen.

"FBI, put your hands up."

The intruder held her in front of him in a chokehold, his automatic pointed at Jackson. "No, you don't," he said, backing out of the doorway.

As soon as they were out, he put her into a fireman's carry and ran down the stairs. His boney shoulder dug into her abdomen, and she prayed he wouldn't trip or she would land on her head.

She heard Jackson clattering down behind them. "Stop! I'll shoot!"

"You wouldn't dare kill this woman, would you?" he hollered.

Just as doors began to open on the other landings, their owners emerging to see what the fuss was, her kidnapper reached the courtyard. He fired in the air. "Get back inside, and you won't get hurt!" he yelled.

He ran across the street and around the corner, where he huddled in the back alley. She was still over his shoulder, and she began pounding on his back with her fists. Then she heard him shoot.

"Agent Jackson!" she screamed.

There was no reply. Meredith kicked up her feet and pounded again with her fists. Before she knew what was happening, her kidnapper had dumped her into the trunk of a car and slammed down the lid. She was trapped.

It took her a few moments before she remembered that she had her phone. Taking it out of the pocket of her jeans, she speed-dialed Aubrey.

"Meredith?" he answered.

"I've been kidnapped. There was an intruder in Allie's condo. He used me as a hostage. Call an ambulance. He shot Agent Jackson in the alley around the corner from Allie's condo, 545 Hinman, Evanston."

"Are you hurt?"

"No. I'm locked in the guy's trunk, and I haven't any idea who he is because he was wearing a ski mask.

"I wish I had my Glock, though," she said. "A lot of good it's doing me sitting at Dick's Sporting Goods. You should be able to trace me with the GPS chip in my phone though, right?"

"The FBI can. Keep it with you whatever you do," he said, his voice terse. "I'll get off the phone, so I can tell Casson to begin the trace."

It was a long drive, wherever they were going. And slow. She guessed her kidnapper didn't dare break the speed limit with her in the trunk. She could make a lot of noise if the police stopped him!

Oddly enough, she wasn't scared. Just angry. She scrabbled about in the enclosed space for a weapon she could use once her kidnapper opened the trunk, but this must be the kind of car that kept the tire repair stuff in a compartment underneath the trunk bed. There was nothing.

Who was her kidnapper? The same person who kidnapped Allie?

But why had he abducted her and where in the world was he taking her?

She was suddenly revolted by the atmosphere in the trunk. Someone had been hauling fertilizer. Ugh.

Meredith tried to conjure up scenarios in her mind showing her to be the heroine in this situation, but she failed.

Was this the man who had been stalking her? Was it Duric? Why would he be in Allie's condo? Was it Allie's father?

Her brain scrambled to make sense of the bunch of facts shooting through her head.

Where was Allie? Where was Stana?

She felt as though her head were going to burst with unanswerable questions, but she kept trying to figure things out in order to keep from thinking about the fire licking at her heels.

An idea sailed into her head. Maybe Aubrey had already thought of it. She called him again.

"Aubrey, have you called Mr. Q? Can you report Allie's and my kidnapping? Get them a picture of me. You should have some on the computer from Bosnia. Actually, there's a picture of Allie and me in her apartment on the credenza in the living room."

"Will do. Hang tight, Meredith. We'll be following."

Finally, she felt the vehicle pull into what sounded like a gravel drive. Her phone said they had been traveling for over an hour.

The kidnapper flipped open the trunk. He stood over her, mask in place, pointing his gun. Seeing her clutching her phone, he grabbed it, swore, and tossed it away into the shrubbery.

"Change of plans," he said, throwing down the trunk lid once again.

This time the drive wasn't as long, but she had no way of telling for certain. Now she began thinking about her mother. Hopefully, Mom was safely ensconced in their cabin on the Upper Peninsula. If anything happened to Meredith, however, no one would know how to get in touch with her mom to tell her. Had she ever even mentioned the cabin to Aubrey? She couldn't remember.

They pulled into what felt like a very long driveway. Once they'd stopped, there was a delay before her captor opened the trunk.

When he did, he handed her a roll of duct tape, still pointing his weapon at her.

"Put it across your mouth."

Grimacing, she did as he asked.

With the weapon still aimed, he yanked her out of the trunk by her arm, making her scramble as best she could. Holding her arm twisted against her back, he marched her into what looked like a gardening hut. Here the smell of fertilizer was even stronger. Unfortunately, it was the organic kind.

Her abductor threw her onto the ground and kept her planted in place with a foot in the small of her back as he duct-taped her wrists behind her. Then, sitting astride her back, he taped her ankles together. When he had finished, he simply walked out of the structure and closed it with the automatic door which came clattering down. She heard him drive away.

CHAPTER EIGHTEEN

Against the advice of Agent Casson, Aubrey left the safe house to meet Agents Marks and Steele at Allie's condo. He had called the police and ambulance, as well. He knew Casson wanted to accompany him, but he needed to stay and guard Aubrey's father.

Aubrey's thoughts were bursting with horrible visions of Meredith locked in a trunk. By the time he reached Evanston from Glen Ellyn, Agent Jackson had been taken to the hospital. According to the police, he was in critical condition, after having suffered a wound to the abdomen.

Marks wouldn't allow him to enter the condo, which was being swept by the scene of the crime techs for prints and other signs of the intruder, but he told him that headquarters was attempting to trace Meredith's phone by her GPS.

"Can you tell what the intruder was looking for?"

"Her office has been tossed. It's impossible to tell."

"Are the photos still there?"

"Let me see," Marks said. "Go back down to the car. I'll come and find you if I get my hands on any photos."

Aubrey simmered with anger at being excluded. With great difficulty, he avoided erupting at Agent Marks, who had to have had little sleep since this drama began. Instead, he went down to the street and paced the sidewalk. When would he hear about Meredith's location? Who was the intruder? Why had he taken Meredith instead of shooting her as he shot Jackson, or even simply running away?

His chest was tight with fear that Meredith might simply be killed and thrown in a dumpster somewhere. His fears were so strong; he could hardly get a grip on himself to focus on what he needed to do. He felt his "black dog" pulling him down, telling him Meredith's situation was hopeless. There was no advantage Aubrey could think of for the abductor to keep her alive.

He thought of her shining eyes when she left tonight. She had been certain she was about to come up with a break in the case. They should have guessed that there might be danger. But Jackson was going with her. The big African-American had certainly appeared to be adequate protection.

This was why he didn't do relationships. Because of his depressive tendencies, he was especially vulnerable to despair, and he needed to try to keep himself on an even keel. It seemed as though all his friends who were involved with women were either in alt or misery. That wasn't the life for him.

But who could keep from loving Meredith? She was not only beautiful with her dark red hair and blue eyes that were so full of fire but could also be so soft with trust. She had been dealt an almost mortal wound with Jan's death, but she chose to continue to live life to its fullest.

His feelings had sneaked up on him. Aubrey knew she had a broken heart and would see any relationship as off-limits for a long time. But the strong heat between them in Bosnia had burnt through both their intentions . . . And they had kissed. Really kissed.

Finally, Marks came down, led him to his car, and after they were seated, handed him a bunch of photos. "I have no way of knowing if any are missing, but here's what I found."

"Thanks. Has anything else turned up?"

"No. Casson caught me up to speed on the fact that you suspect Allie's father might have been a Croatian war criminal," said Marks. "And your experiment down in Lansing bore fruit. An undercover bowler, huh? And you even got a name. So, bottom line is we're looking for another Serbian war criminal working in cahoots with Duric who might have kidnapped your mom? Seems like we're knee deep in war criminals suddenly."

"It is odd. I don't know why anyone would want to kidnap Allie," said Aubrey. "And if her abductor was the same man who took Meredith, did he even know who Meredith was when he kidnapped her? Are we talking about two cases here, or are they somehow connected?"

"Put that way it does sound like a longshot," said Marks.

"But we can't worry about the why at the moment," said Aubrey. There was a frozen ball of terror in his gut. "Our first priority has to be finding Meredith before they decide to get rid of her."

"Yeah. Of course," agreed the agent.

"I'll go ahead and look through these photos," Aubrey said, "But it's probably useless because if the intruder were after one of them, he would have taken it. "I need to call my boss."

He called Mr. Q. "Sir, I'm sorry to tell you, but this story just got more dangerous. Meredith's best friend, Allie Novak, got kidnapped in Evanston. We're sending you her picture. This may or may not have to do with the case. She was born in Bosnia. Her father's a reclusive Croatian named Mikal Novak."

"Sounds like there should be a connection to the case somehow."

"We don't know as yet, but while Meredith and an FBI agent were looking through the apartment for clues to her disappearance, Agent Jackson was shot. He's been taken to the hospital, and now Meredith has been kidnapped. We are tracing her with the GPS on her phone."

Mr. Q swore. "Not Meredith! This thing is like an octopus sprouting tentacles. I have to hurry to get this on the 10 o'clock news."

The agent came back down and handed Aubrey the photo of Allie and Meredith which he snapped a picture of by the light of the car's indoor lamp and sent it off to Mr. Q.

The agent's phone chimed. "Yes. Yeah. Thanks. Got it." Marks hung up. "That was headquarters. Good news. They have a location for Meredith. They traced her north to Lake Geneva. Maybe someone's summer home. They want Steele and me to go in."

"I'm coming with you," said Aubrey.

"Listen, there's no telling what we're going to find. It could be dangerous. In fact, it probably will be dangerous. I can't have you going off half-cocked."

"I promise I won't do that. I'll follow your directions. I can't sit here any longer wondering what's happened to her."

"All right," said Marks. "But when I tell you to stay in the car, stay in the car."

* * *

On the drive north, Aubrey couldn't keep himself from asking, "Why do you think he took her? He shot Agent Jackson. Why didn't he shoot her?"

Agent Steele answered, "To be frank, it's puzzling. We think he may be using her as a hostage. Have you looked at the photos yet?"

"Yeah, there's nothing but scenery," said Aubrey. "On her trip to the Caribbean there are some party shots around a pool, but only Allie would know who the people were."

"He could have found a picture and taken it away with him."

"I guess that could be it. But I've been thinking," said Aubrey. "What if it was Allie's dad and he was after the letter he left her? The one you have."

"How would her dad know she had been kidnapped? We haven't been able to get a hold of him," said Marks.

There was a moment's silence. Aubrey fought off the blackness of the night they were passing through. It felt like a physical thing, an ominous thing. The absence of all light. Depression clamped down on him. He forced himself to surface.

Finally, they reached Lake Geneva.

"The location of her phone isn't really specific, other than being somewhere on this property.

"There's a house. Behind those trees," said Aubrey.

"I see it," said Agent Steele. "It looks like it's the only one in the area."

They pulled up, and both agents reminded him that he was to stay in the car. Both agents put on Kevlar vests and got assault rifles out of the trunk.

Aubrey toyed with the idea of calling Meredith's phone, but decided if her kidnapper didn't know she had it, Aubrey's call would give her away.

Through the moonless night, he could hardly make out the agents as they stood at the front door. After a few moments, they walked away from the front porch. It looked as though they were knocking at windows.

He supposed they needed a warrant to go inside without permission. He hadn't thought of that. If the kidnapper were inside, he would realize this, of course, and decide to move her before they came back with a warrant.

His heart slipped a little further into the Black Hole of Calcutta.

The agents returned to the car. "No car in the garage. No response to our knocks at the door or on the windows."

"Maybe there's another house in the area."

"We can look," said Agent Murphy.

But looking around within the boundaries of Meredith's GPS signal, revealed no house or shed where she could be kept.

"Would you mind going back to the house?" Aubrey asked. "I'll call her phone. It's got to be somewhere around here."

"It's worth a try," said Agent Murphy.

They had reached the house. He stepped out of the car and called Meredith's phone. He heard it ringing!

Following the sound, he walked through the small wooded area to the west of the house. All at once, he realized what this could mean. Was he going to find Meredith's corpse?

It was a relief when he finally found her phone with the aid of the agents' flashlight. It was sitting, all alone at the base of a birch tree.

"Well," said Agent Murphy, "This could mean a number of things. She threw it away to let us know she was here. Or the kidnapper realized she had it, threw it away, and then took her somewhere else where he was off the boundaries of her phone signal."

"We have to find out who owns this house," said Aubrey. "It's probably just a summer home like you said."

"That'll have to wait 'til the morning. But this phone gives us probable cause that she has been taken against her will and might be in that house. We can legally enter using force."

Aubrey started to follow them, but they waved him back to the car. He stood watching as they broke a window pane next to the door, reached in and unlocked the door from the inside. An alarm went off as they opened the door, but they paid no heed. Entering, they were lost to Aubrey's sight. He didn't realize he was holding his breath until he felt his lungs about to explode.

After at least a lifetime had passed, the two agents exited the house. "No one there," Steele called to him. "After he realized she had a phone, he must have taken her somewhere else."

"You can find out who owns this property, right?" asked Aubrey.

"Right. But not tonight. Let's find a motel or something and get some sleep," said Steele. "After we make our report, of course. In it we'll put an urgent request to find the homeowner first thing in the morning. With three kidnappings, they're going to be putting a lot more people on this case. Probably a team for each crime."

* * *

Even though he was exhausted, with his mother and Meredith missing, Aubrey was wound far too tightly for sleep. Obsessing over what few disparate facts they possessed got him nowhere. They needed a break. Taking out the pictures, he looked through them again. Nothing. The only ones with any people in them just showed a bunch of shirtless men and bikini-clad women by a pool. In the distance was the turquoise blue of Caribbean waters. Meredith had said Allie had been visiting the Caymans.

Maybe the intruder/kidnapper *had* been after the letter, which argued that he was Allie's father. What would the county tax records tell them about the owner of the house in Lake Geneva?

So much had happened to him in such a short space of time, Aubrey was having difficulty keeping his facts straight. Using the small pad of paper the Fairfield Inn provided, he made three separate lists:

Mom's kidnapping—Duric's confederate (Drasko Subotic?)

- *To use as a hostage?*
- *Why hadn't they heard from the kidnapper?*
- *To humiliate and hurt my mother physically, possibly to kill her.*

Allie's kidnapping—?

- *For money?*
- *To manipulate Allie's father?*

Meredith's kidnapping—Allie's Father?

- *Opportunistic—using her as a shield at the scene*
- *Fear she would recognize him as Allie's father*
- *To trade for Allie????*

When Aubrey's exhausted brain had compiled his lists, he lay down on his bed and had no further intellectual barriers to the emotions that were overtaking him.

I love my mother. I love Meredith. I've got to find a way to save them.

Futility assailed him. It had been a long time since he had felt those awful tentacles grasping him and carrying him to that place where there was no light.

He made himself get off the bed and turned on all the lights in his motel room. He turned on the television, and shunning the news channels, he watched a classic movie channel, trying to lose himself in visions of Bogart and Bacall, Cary Grant and Deborah Kerr. He drank all the juice in the mini-fridge and left the alcohol alone.

CHAPTER NINETEEN

Meredith was lying on cement, and it was cold. She tried to roll into a ball to conserve energy, but it was difficult with her arms behind her back. The idea of all the creatures that might be crawling on or around her made her nauseous. Beneath the smell of fertilizer was the odor of potting soil.

Gardening shears. *Hmm.* Not likely to do her much good with her hands behind her, even if she could see to find them. There must be something she could do!

Was Agent Jackson dead? Who was the guy in the ski mask? What had he been looking for?

The obvious answer was the photographs. Had he had a chance to grab them? She knew Aubrey would study them in detail if he had a chance.

She also knew she shouldn't stop at the obvious. Maybe it hadn't been the photos. Maybe the man in the ski mask was Mr. Novak and he was looking for the letter he had written to Allie. She didn't think it, by itself, was terribly incriminating, but the contents of the safety deposit box might be.

And where was Allie? Why had *she* been kidnapped?

Unbidden, came memories of late nights spent together in their room trying to study for finals. They were both Nutella freaks. They had the biggest size jar you could buy and experimented with all different sort of ways you could eat it. Once, when they were living in an apartment, they had even melted it and, with a few other spices added, made a sauce for chicken breasts. They were going to write a cookbook someday called *The Nutella Challenge—101 Ways to Cook with Nutella.*

The memory brought tears to her eyes and she wept for her friend. Why would anyone want to kill Allie?

She could see why people might want to kidnap Meredith Montgomery, Investigative Journalist—after all she was up to her neck in evidence against Zoran

Duric. He had threatened her with death already. Thinking of the newspaper photo with its red slash, she shivered.

And where was Stana?

Thinking of Aubrey and Dr. Kettering, her heart almost broke. She could tell Stana's husband worshipped her. And Aubrey had experienced a wonderful childhood at her side. Who had kidnapped her? Was it a cohort of Duric? It had to be, didn't it?

Duric was so obviously psychopathic; she knew she couldn't even imagine all the evils he had committed in his life.

To expunge the man and her fears from her mind, she disciplined herself to think of Aubrey. In almost every way, she knew Aubrey better than she had ever known Jan. And Jan hadn't known her like Aubrey did. Jan had thought her high-minded and selfless. Each day of their life together had been full of service to others. She had thought of him more as a saint than as a human being with his share of foibles.

By contrast, her days with Aubrey had been fairly ordinary until they began to work on this story together. Then, their relationship had been built layer by layer—as they made discoveries, as she met his family, and as he protected her from threats. Next came the pressure cooker: Bosnia—where they had run for their lives. And now, this new crisis: his mother's kidnapping. They had taken the worst life had to offer and had lived through it together.

So far.

Neither one of them was selfless or perfect. Right now, for instance, she was worried sick that Aubrey was putting his life at risk. But that was what he did. Doubtless, he was cooking up some scheme to rescue her that would be full of danger to himself.

She had to get out of here before he could put such a scheme into play. Morning might bring possibilities if there was a window in this place. Windows had glass and glass could cut through duct tape. Or she might find a garden implement that would serve the same purpose. Meredith was reasonably certain that once it was light, she could find some way of undoing her bonds.

On that resolution, surprisingly, she slept.

CHAPTER TWENTY

True light emerged for Aubrey in the form of morning and agents pounding on the door.

"Your mother has escaped. She's waiting for us at headquarters," said Agent Steele.

Too stunned to cover his reactions, Aubrey's body shook, and he felt tears in his eyes.

* * *

When Aubrey arrived with Special Agents Murphy and Steele at FBI headquarters, he leaped from the car like a jack-in-the-box, despite having had no sleep. He ran inside the building but was forced to wait for the agents to get him past reception.

Finally, he arrived at the victim's first-aid clinic where his mother sat, rumpled and weary-looking with a bruise on her chin and an IV in her arm. A smile spread over her face, and she came to her feet when Aubrey walked into the room. Agent Marks stood by her.

"My darling boy," she said in her native tongue as she hugged him to her.

He answered her, holding her close to him. "Mom," was all he could say. Now the tears ran down his face. In Serbo-Croatian, he said, "I didn't think I would ever see you alive again. How did you ever escape?"

"Could I trouble you to speak in English?" asked Marks. "I know this is an emotional time, but anything you say could be important."

"Who kidnapped you? What did they do to your face? Are you hurt anywhere else?" Aubrey demanded.

"Sit down, Aubrey," his mother said. He detected weariness in her stance as she swayed a little.

They both sat, but he retained her hand.

"I don't know who took me. I don't think he planned for me to live, for he let me see his face. I didn't know him. But he spoke Serbo-Croatian."

"How did he take you?"

"I was working in the garden. No one was around. He crept up behind me and used chloroform. At least I think that's what I think it was."

"Where did he take you?"

"To a crummy hotel by the airport. He ripped out the telephone cord in the room, put a do not disturb sign on the door, and left me tied up on the bed with duct tape over my mouth and around my wrists and ankles. I never saw him again."

She went on, "My brother came straight to the hotel from his trip back to Bosnia. He greeted me with a smile and a fist to my face. Then he ripped off the tape across my mouth." She gulped and lowered her eyes. "Oh, Aubrey, he spoke foul things. He told me he had killed you in Bosnia, that he had blown you up. He described it with many details. He said he was only waiting to capture your father; then he was going to have me watch while he killed him, too."

"Oh, *Majko*!" Aubrey leaped up from his chair and bent down to caress her bruised face. His own face ached as though the blow had been struck there. "I can't stand it that he treated you this way. But you escaped from him. Did they give you any food? Any water?"

"No."

Aubrey turned on Agent Marks. "You have taken care of that, I hope."

"First thing," said the nurse. She has been thoroughly checked out and given plenty to drink. She's on that IV to replace her electrolytes and saline. She hasn't wanted to eat. She was too worried about you and your dad."

"You told her I wasn't dead? That Dad was in a safe house?"

"Of course. First thing."

"Oh, Aubrey," his mother said, crying now. "You cannot imagine how relieved I was!" Surging to her feet again, she embraced him once more, laying her face against his chest and holding him to her with feverish desperation. "My son, my son."

"I am all right, *Majko*." He hugged her back, hard. "It just makes me feel murderous to know how badly he treated you. How did you get away from Duric?"

"When he left, he didn't tape my mouth again. I think he loved hearing me plead with him too much. I rolled off the bed and over to the door. I cried for help with all my might through the space under the door. One of the maids opened it and screamed when she saw me. Then she ran for the manager.

"He couldn't believe it when he saw me. After he cut through the tapes, he moved me to another room, and I told him to call the FBI and mention that I was your mother."

"I'm sure you startled him plenty," said Aubrey. Turning to Agent Marks, he said, "I suppose they have someone waiting in the hotel room to intercept Duric?"

"He hasn't shown up there. I don't know what tipped him off. Maybe he saw the agents leading her out downstairs in the hotel."

"And my father?"

"He should be here any minute. We are taking them both back to the safe house, but we want to make certain Mrs. Kettering is all right. Going so long without water is hard on the body." At that moment the door to Agent Marks office opened and Aubrey smelled breakfast.

"I ordered it for you and your mother," said Agent Steele. Motioning toward her partner, she said, "We'll leave you alone while we go down to the cafeteria."

Just as the agents were leaving, Aubrey's father burst through the door, "Stana! My darling!"

Aubrey got out of the way and enjoyed watching the reunion between his parents. This time his mother's tears were voluble and not easily checked. His tall father wrapped his wife in his arms and put his cheek against the top of her head. "My darling, darling girl. I am so glad you are all right."

Wondering if a reunion with Meredith would be part of his future, he tried to believe it would be. Aubrey attacked the pancakes, eggs, and bacon while his mother repeated her story. At length, his father turned to him and said, "Meredith? Allie? Any news on them?"

"What has happened to your Meredith?" asked his mother. "And who is Allie?"

Aubrey was reluctant to dampen his mother's joy. "They have been kidnapped, as well."

He hoped Agent Marks had an ownership trace in process for the house in Lake Geneva.

Something else nagged at his mind, but he was so tired he couldn't get hold of it. He went back to his orange juice.

"*Majko*, you must eat something. Have some juice, at least. Dad is here now. You have no more worries."

"But I worry for Meredith now. And this Allie?"

"Allie is Meredith's best friend. Oddly enough, we just discovered that her father is also probably a war criminal. Croatian."

"How strange," his mother said.

"Have you ever heard the name Drasko Subotic?" he asked.

"Yes," said his mother. "You don't need to worry about him. He went back to Bosnia and was killed by an assassin."

Aubrey deflated. "You are sure of this?"

"Bilijana wrote me when it happened, because he had caused a big stir in our church community, and I had written her about him at the time. When he was assassinated, she thought I would be interested."

"So much for my brilliant detective work. I guess it would have been too easy. I thought he might be Allie's father. He goes by the name of Mikal Novak here."

"Why was Allie kidnapped?" asked Aubrey of no one in particular.

When the Special Agents returned, Marks was pessimistic about getting a warrant for Allie's father's safety deposit box. "Unless we can prove for certain that he was a wanted war criminal, I doubt we can even get a warrant to search his house. His daughter's been kidnapped. He's a sympathetic party in this case."

"I bet you a buck, he was at Allie's condo last night searching for that letter we found. And that would make him Meredith's kidnapper."

"That sounds good, except that the letter really wasn't that damning. He just lets his daughter know he wasn't a saint during the war and says he loves her. I don't think that would cut it with a judge," said Marks.

Aubrey turned toward his mother. "Mom, would you be willing to work with a sketch artist to come up with a face of your kidnapper when you're settled in the safe house?"

"Of course," she said. "I want that pig-person caught. Especially, if he might be Meredith's kidnapper, too. I am worried about your sweetheart, darling."

He didn't correct his mother about Meredith's status. After all, there was that kiss.

CHAPTER TWENTY-ONE

The sketch artist arrived at the safe house later that afternoon. A new idea had come to Aubrey. He was anxious to see if it would bear fruit. A great deal depended upon his mother's memory and the accuracy of the sketch that the artist would render.

He showered, shaved, and dressed in a pair of clean jeans. Aubrey made a big lunch—sandwiches, salad, even some smoothies. Did Meredith even have food? Probably not.

Taking his mother's lunch to her where she sat with the artist in the dining room, he had a look at the sketch.

Nope. To his knowledge, he hadn't seen the guy. But maybe his dad had.

However, when his dad came downstairs after his shower, he didn't recognize the sketch either.

Aubrey broached his idea to Agent Marks who was back at the house with them this afternoon. "Do you think we could get whatever evidence the Hague already has about Duric and any of his known associates e-mailed over to us today? If this man kidnapped my mother on orders from Duric, they have to have a connection. From what I understand the Bosnian Serbians fought in paramilitary cadres that just sprang up. They could have been in the same cadre."

"Yes," his mother said. "That's true. And my brother was the leader of such a band when they were fighting in Zvornik. Excellent idea, darling."

Agent Marks agreed and said he would put in a call to headquarters in D.C. immediately. They would take care of it. Before he left the room, he tore a sheet off his tablet and placed it on the table in front of Aubrey's lunch. "This just came in. It's the owner of the property you asked about in Lake Geneva."

"Fantastic! That should lead us somewhere useful," said Aubrey. "I need to phone Mr. Q and tell him about my mother's escape. He will want plenty of details. Is it okay for me to release them?"

"Definitely. We want as much public sympathy and co-operation as we can get. Show the sketch. Be sure to put up our tip line. Murphy and Casson are out at the hotel room where your mom was kept trying to come up with trace evidence—DNA or fingerprints. We have another team out at the Lake Geneva house, taking it apart."

"Good. How is Agent Jackson this morning?"

"Last report, he is out of surgery, and they are guardedly optimistic."

"I'll tell my boss that, too." Aubrey left the room for the little den where he had spent so much time with Meredith. Closing his eyes, he took in a deep breath to steady his nerves. Then he made the call.

Mr. Q was grateful that Aubrey was taking him inside the investigation. He was tremendously pleased about his mother's escape.

"I know that to you this is life and death," said Aubrey's boss. "But it's top notch journalism."

"Anything on the tip line?"

"One of the neighbors saw Meredith thrown in the trunk. They didn't get the license plate, but the car was late model Cadillac. Gold."

"The FBI knows this?"

"Yes. I called it in."

"Thanks, Mr. Q. I've got a line to pursue now, so I'll let you know if anything comes of it."

CHAPTER TWENTY-TWO

When Meredith woke on a dirty cement floor, it took a moment for her to realize where she was. She had been dreaming blissfully of Paris. Reality clamped down on her like a vice.

Water. I've got to have some water.

But, even if there were a source in this shed, her mouth, hands, and feet were taped. Her head throbbed with thirst. Her body was cold and stiff. Why hadn't the intruder simply shot her?

She couldn't think that way. She was alive, and her life was a gift.

Looking around her in the feeble light from one small window, she saw that she was right about being in a gardening shed. Large flower pots sat around her on the floor, along with a riding lawnmower, a Rototiller, and a leaf-blower. Rakes, brooms, and other smaller implements hung on the walls.

What can I do with what I have here?

The first thing she needed to do was to sit up. Using her stomach muscles, her feet, and her hands, she managed this, although it was painful. Shaking her head, she tossed her hair out of her eyes.

The window was chest high. If she was going to see out of it, or more importantly, break it, she needed to stand. To do that, she needed to be near a wall. She set about scooting on her behind, using her heels as traction.

For the first time, she noted some shelves bolted to the wall in a darker part of the shed. Ideal for helping her to stand up. Scooting over to them took a toll on her abdominal muscles, not to mention the seat of her pants, but she paid no attention. Who knew how long it would be before her captor returned?

When she finally reached the shelves, she maneuvered herself, so her back was to them. Flexing her arms, she clenched her fists and, anchoring her knuckles on a shelf, steadied herself, and tried to rise. It wasn't easy. In fact, it was very awkward. She was able to rise a bit, then wedge her hips on the edge of a shelf, and move up her hands to a higher shelf until she was finally standing.

She promptly fell straight forward. At the last moment, she twisted, landing on her shoulder and banging the side of her head on the concrete. That was the last thing she knew.

CHAPTER TWENTY-THREE

Aubrey looked at the ownership documentation for the Lake Geneva house on his computer screen. A real estate trust. Undoubtedly, it was the bolt hole for someone. Their safe place where they supposedly couldn't be traced through property tax records.

But they didn't know who they were dealing with. So far, he'd had no need to use his particular strengths in this case, but now, perhaps they would come in handy. Aubrey was a hacker par excellence. He had serious skills.

The trust was actually a red flag. What self-respecting criminal would put property in his own name?

Sitting down in the kitchen at his laptop, Aubrey mentally flexed his hacking muscles. Now. Who was the trustee for this piece of property? Mr. Packer A. Fortnum. Nice. Very distinctive.

He looked Mr. Fortnum up online.

Ah! Mr. Packer A. Fortnum was a partner at Williams, Weir, and Dodge, one of the more enormous firms in Chicago. Now came the fun part: hacking into the firm's digital records. In his experience, he'd found that firms that size digitized everything.

He set up his password hacker software and let it work. Opening another screen, he looked up more background on Mr. Fortnum. The man was ninety-eight and still practicing law! He had an impeccable résumé Educated at Cornell. Rhodes Scholar. Ah! This was interesting. He had fought with Tito in World War II and therefore probably spoke Serbo-Croatian. Harvard Law School. Started at the firm in 1950.

His software hacker arrived at the password an hour later. After that, it was just plain fun.

Because of how the Lake Geneva house was featured in this case, he imagined that its owner might have been of Bosnian descent. Aubrey zeroed in on the years 1992-2000—the war and post-war years. The property description was long, so he just used the county and lot number to search.

This yielded a nice little packet of documents. The house was purchased in 1995. The original trust naming Fortnum as the trustee was replaced by a document recorded the next day. It named Mr. Anthony Sepastopol as the new trustee, which was disappointing, but Aubrey pressed on. Eventually, he found a page of digitized notes. The notes were a reminder to Fortnum from himself that he needed to draw up a DBA form for none other than Zoran Duric doing business as Anthony Sebastopol. Aubrey couldn't find that Fortnum had ever followed through. But the information he needed was there.

Zoran Duric owned the house in Lake Geneva. Unbelievable. But there it was.

His mind went back to the newspaper photo with the red line canceling Meredith's face. A wave of heat followed by chills ran through Aubrey, and he felt like he was going to throw up. Zoran Duric had his hands on the woman Aubrey loved, and he had threatened to kill her.

But what had Duric been doing at Allie's condo? What was he searching for?

If there was one thing he was positive of, it was that Allie did not know Duric, so what was the connection? Had Duric kidnapped Allie, too? Why?

He walked into the living room to find Agents Marks and Steele, both on their laptops.

He explained what he had found out. "Allie Novak's kidnapping has something to do with the Duric case. The man who was caught searching Allie's condo initially took Meredith to a house owned by Duric in Lake Geneva. It may have been Duric himself."

"What?" Marks said.

"I know. It makes no sense. I was sitting right next to Allie when Meredith asked her if she knew if her father knew Duric. She said he never talked about any of that stuff. Meaning the war. Allie was totally uninterested."

"I am less concerned with that, than with the fact that Meredith may be in Duric's hands, Aubrey. This is bad news," said Agent Steele.

"I'm aware of that. He threatened to kill her." Aubrey was sweating as though he had run a marathon.

"I am sending a team out to go through that house with a fine-toothed comb. Then we'll keep it under surveillance. Does he own any other properties in the Chicago area?"

"Good question. He used a DBA for that one. I'll check and see if there are any others listed under that name."

A further search of Cook County and all the counties surrounding it showed no one named Anthony Sebastopol or Zoran Duric as owning property. The search took some time, and while Aubrey had initially been hopeful, his hope waned and then flickered out at his failure to turn up anything.

At about four o'clock the files came through from the Hague by way of Marks, who forwarded them to him. Disheartened by his failure to locate any more property owned by Duric, he was anxious for this new project and tackled it gladly.

The Hague had sent a list of known associates in Duric's paramilitary unit accompanied by digitized photos. None of them matched the drawing made by the sketch artist that morning, which was yet another disappointment. However, the file also indicated that all these men had been caught, successfully prosecuted, and were serving long sentences in prison, so, of course, none of them was the man he was looking for.

Hoping for information of any kind, he read the history of the unit as the prosecution team had pieced it together.

> *Ludi Sakali (mad jackals) was formed in 1992 from Bosnian Serbian radicals in Zoran Duric's neighborhood in Sarajevo. Though they were anti-Croatian, their primary animus was against the Bosniaks. They went about looting and defacing mosques throughout the country, murdering Imams and faithful followers as they worshipped.*
>
> *Their worst excesses were committed at Zvornik. Transcriptions of witnesses' testimonies are attached.*
>
> *Members of Ludi Sakali were initiated into the paramilitary group by receiving a small tattoo of a jackal baring his teeth. The mark is located on the upper right region of their backs over the shoulder blade.*

Aubrey read through the transcriptions attached. They were sickeningly graphic and reminded him far too much of the testimonies he had gathered in Sarajevo. His determination to seize Duric grew until it almost choked him. Thinking of Meredith in his hands was more than he could bear.

Aubrey sat in a deep funk looking at his blank computer. Duric owned property in the States. He had bought it in 1995. But he had been living in Vienna, according to EUFOR. How had he paid his property taxes? Where had the bill gone?

He sat upright and slid a hand down his face, as though he could wipe away his exhaustion. Public record. Those things were a matter of public record.

Going online to the County Assessor's records, he typed in the city and lot number. For the year 2017, the bill had been sent to Mr. Mikal Novak, 2067 Larkspur Lane, Lake Forest, Illinois.

Allie's father. The Croatian. He was connected to Duric somehow.

But the how of things wasn't important now. What was important was that Novak had probably acted as a caretaker of sorts and had keys to the Lake Geneva property. As Novak saw it, the perfect place to stash Meredith. Until her stunt with the phone.

Yes. It was more likely that *he* had been the intruder at his daughter's condo looking for the letter he had left for her not to be opened until his death. So, it followed that he was the more likely kidnapper.

Where would he have taken Meredith after the discovery of her phone altered his plans? The Lake Forest house. Aubrey went for Agent Marks. This called for backup.

* * *

Aubrey had been worried they would need a warrant, but after he provided Marks with the paper trail leading to Novak, the agent considered it probable cause to inspect the Lake Forest property to look for Meredith. He ran it by the Agent in Charge just to be sure.

The drive to Lake Forest took way too long.

"No one has shown up at the Lake Geneva house, I take it?" Aubrey asked Agent Marks who was accompanied by Steele.

"No. Meredith's phone spooked them, I'm guessing. They know we have our eye on the place."

"If Meredith isn't on the Lake Forest property, I don't know where to look," said Aubrey.

"One thing at a time, Aubrey," said Marks. "One thing at a time."

When they finally reached the property on Larkspur Lane, they parked a couple of blocks down the street. Local police had barricaded both ends of the lane, and several stood at attention in front of the house as the agents and Aubrey approached the house from the opposite curb. Marks had his weapon out of his shoulder holster.

The house was covered in ivy and large enough for a big family. In the dark, it looked threatening and suitably spooky.

Using her flashlight, Agent Steele went around to the back of the house to stand by the back door.

When they had given her enough time to get in place, Aubrey and Marks approached the deep front porch, climbed the steps and rang the doorbell. A Hispanic maid answered.

"I am sorry. Mr. Novak is not at home."

Marks showed his creds. "We have reason to believe that he has kidnapped a woman named Meredith Montgomery and that he is holding her in this house."

The maid's eyes grew large. "I would know if there was a woman in this house. There is not."

Marks pushed past her. "I think we'll just have a look for ourselves."

Running past Marks and the maid, Aubrey raced up the stairs. He flung one door open after another. No Meredith.

He tried the closets. No luck there either. He was just climbing up the stairs to the attic when Marks joined him. The attic was poorly lit, but a careful search yielded no Meredith.

Aubrey's heart was in his feet. Kicking aside shoeboxes and suitcases, he went over to the dormer window which looked out over the property. Security lights shone from the detached garage and another small building.

Throwing open the window, he shouted down to Agent Steele, "What's that other building with the lights on it?"

"I'll check it out," she called back.

He waited what seemed like an eternity, watching as the flashlight seemed to bobble across the lawn.

"It's a shed," she called up.

Hope sprang in him anew, and he made for the stairs. Heart pounding, he raced through the kitchen to the back door.

Aubrey ran across the lawn, reaching the shed in moments.

"The only access is an automatic garage door," said Agent Steele. "I've tried all the obvious codes, but it won't open."

Aubrey was skirting the shed. "There's a window here. Can you give me your flashlight?"

Using the heavy instrument, he knocked out the glass. He aimed the flashlight into the shed and began inspecting the floor.

He saw Meredith's body sprawled on the floor. She must be unconscious or even dead not to have heard the noise they were making. "Yup. She's there."

Fueled by adrenaline, Aubrey began knocking out the rest of the window. Then he took off his jacket and covered the edge of the windowsill where tiny spikes of glass remained.

"Wait," Agent Steele said. "You'll never make it through there. I'll go. Sometimes it's an advantage to be small. There will be a garage door opener button in there."

Using the stirrup Aubrey formed with his hands, the woman hoisted herself up and through the window. He could only watch as she approached Meredith.

"There's a pulse," she announced. "Toss me the flashlight, and I'll get that door open."

Aubrey hadn't realized he'd been holding his breath until he exhaled with a whoosh. "Thank the Lord," he said softly, tossing her the flashlight.

In a moment, he heard the creak of the lumbering garage door as it opened. Agent Marks was now running toward them across the lawn.

They both entered the dank shed. Aubrey approached Meredith carefully in the dim shed. "She's lying kind of funny," he said, testing for himself to see that she had a pulse. It seemed normal. "Better call an ambulance."

As Agent Steele did this, he carefully moved Meredith's auburn hair out of her face. He stared down at her. He had been so afraid he would never see her again. She had to be all right. It had been a miracle that they had found her.

Agent Marks was busy photographing Meredith as she lay. As soon as he was finished, Aubrey pulled the duct tape off her mouth and began working on her hands and ankle restraints.

Meredith remained unconscious. He longed to gather her to him and cradle her, but he didn't dare move her until they found out if anything was broken.

It seemed forever before the ambulance arrived and drove across the back lawn to the shed, as Agent Steele had instructed them. Paramedics poured out of the back of the vehicle in their orange suits and rushed to them, carrying a stretcher. Reluctantly, Aubrey moved aside.

After assuring that her pulse was all right, they fitted her with a neck brace and moved her onto a backboard which they slid onto the stretcher. Once they had her inside the vehicle, they checked her for wounds and fitted her out with an oxygen mask.

"There's a large contusion on the side of her head," one EMT reported. "We'll need to get her to the hospital to x-ray her. That is most likely the reason she is unconscious. Her vital signs are okay."

"Where's the nearest hospital?" asked Aubrey.

"Here in Lake Forest. Northwestern Medical has a branch hospital here. They've got a top-rated ER. Don't worry."

"Can I ride with her?" he asked.

"There's room for one of you," the EMT said.

For the first time, Agent Marks showed his creds. "We'll arrange for backup to meet us here, and then we'll come to the hospital. She's a kidnap victim."

* * *

In the curtained alcove of the ER, Aubrey sat next to Meredith after they had x-rayed her skull. He held her hand and waited, praying with his might to the God he knew for her to wake up.

It was too early for them to call her situation a coma, and the doctor had told him that she had didn't have a skull fracture. Apparently, her shoulder had taken the brunt of the fall. But her head was packed in ice to stem the bleeding. No one knew how long she had been lying there in the shed with her injury.

How had it happened? Had Mikal Novak dumped her into that shed on her head intentionally? Or was Duric the kidnapper? It was over twenty-four hours since one of them had taken her. What had they planned to do to her? Starve her to death?

She was on an IV already for fluids. Her face, the filth on it washed away, was white against her vibrant hair. All except the strip across her mouth which was red and swollen from where the duct tape had been eased off. He studied the hand that he held, tracing her veins with his finger. *Keep flowing, blood.*

"You've got to rally, Meredith. You've just got to. We need to catch these monsters. Who knows what they are up to? And what about Allie? We have to find Allie.

"Did you see the face of the man who kidnapped you? Who was it?

"Okay. I'll tell you the truth. I know you don't want me to, but I can't help myself. I love you anyway. How could I not? You are the only bright thing in my life right now. I want to protect you, to show you God can be good in spite of the tragedy you suffered. I want to take you back to Paris. I think that is where it began for me. Loving you. You are so earnest, so concerned for the Bosnians, my people. For some crazy reason, you are drawn to them. Could you, by any chance, be drawn to me in particular?"

Her head began to thrash back and forth. "Jan?" she asked in a croaky voice.

His heart dropped. Then her eyes opened.

"Oh," she said, her eyes strangely unfocused. He could see that one pupil was larger than the other. "It's you, Aubrey. Where am I?"

"You're in the hospital in Lake Forest. We found you in Mikal Novak's garden shed. Do you remember anything that happened?"

"Mikal Novak? Allie's father?"

"We figure it was either he or Duric who kidnapped you. Do you remember any of it?"

"Not much. I spent the whole time in the trunk of his car."

"Did you see his face?"

"No. But why would Allie's father kidnap me?"

"You interrupted him when he was searching Allie's condo. He shot Agent Jackson but took you as hostage."

"Is the agent dead?"

"No. He's going to pull through, but it was a near thing. If you hadn't called 911, he would have bled out before anyone found him."

"My phone! Did you find my phone?"

"Yes." He told her about the house owned by Duric and an abbreviated version of the research that had led to their finding her. "I'm just sorry it took so long. I guess you should press your call button. The nurse will be glad you are awake."

CHAPTER TWENTY-FOUR

Meredith's head and shoulder were hurting so much she didn't think she could tolerate the pain. It was the same shoulder she had dislocated in Bosnia. But she was extremely grateful to be alive. Her struggle in the shed was coming back to her.

As a sour-looking nurse questioned and examined her, Aubrey was asked to leave the cubicle.

"You have a severe concussion, Ms. Montgomery. And your clavicle is fractured. Your shoulder was dislocated, but the doctor was able to move it back into position and set your clavicle while you were unconscious. That's why you have the sling."

"I'm lucky," she told the nurse. "It hurts like blazes, but I could just as easily be dead."

"Well, the FBI is waiting to question you. I can give you over-the-counter meds for the pain, but nothing stronger until we are sure you're not going to lapse into a coma. Like I said, your concussion is severe."

"I'll take the meds. The sooner, the better, please. And you may send the agents in."

"Are you sure?"

"Very sure," Meredith said. "And I'd like Aubrey to be in here, too."

The nurse pursed her lips but finally left the cubicle to do as she asked.

* * *

"I remembered," she said as soon as she saw Aubrey. "I thought there was no way anyone was going to be able to figure out where I was. I thought I'd have to rescue myself."

She told him of her aborted attempt to stand. "I would have fallen flat on my face, but I managed to twist at the last moment."

"Your wits didn't completely desert you, then. But how could you ever doubt my ability to find you?" He tapped on an invisible keyboard. "I'm the best."

"You are," she said with a sad smile.

"And I had a little help from my Friend upstairs."

"So, it is literally, thank heavens."

"Yes."

Special Agents Marks and Steele entered the cubicle.

"It's good to see you, Meredith," he said.

She responded, "Hi. It's good to see another female. I can't see my hands. Are they dirty?"

Agent Steele laughed. "A little. After seeing that filthy shed, I don't blame you for being concerned. Would you like me to wash them for you?

"Yes, please."

There was a sink in the cubicle and a stack of paper towels. Using warm water, Agent Steele washed her hands. Aubrey passed her a container of hand sanitizer that was sitting on the sink.

Meredith sighed with relief.

During the next bit, she grew progressively more exhausted, and the pain in her head and shoulder increased exponentially. Aubrey finally called a stop to the questioning. It was obvious, to him at least, that she knew nothing more than what she had said.

"That's enough, agents. I think the only thing she's been able to tell us is that he spoke English without an accent. That argues for Novak. Let's allow her to get some sleep now."

"Has anyone come back to the house where I was?" she asked.

"No one has been reported," said Agent Marks. "Police are staking it out from a block away, I understand."

"A big house with ivy all over it?"

"Yes. You know it?"

"Allie took me home once to meet her father. It was about four years ago, I think."

"So, you've seen the man? That could be a tremendous help. No wonder he didn't take off his ski mask."

"But he's Croatian, not Serbian," she protested.

"Well, whatever he is, he's working with Duric. That was his house Novak took you to in the first place," Agent Marks said.

"It's strange. Serbians killed Allie's mother. And who kidnapped Allie?"

"Maybe Duric is blackmailing the man, using his daughter," said Agent Steele.

"That's possible, I guess," mused Meredith.

"We'll leave you to get some rest," said Agent Marks. "But if you remember anything, have Aubrey call us."

"Good-bye," said Meredith. "And thanks for helping Aubrey rescue me, Agent Steele."

She smiled and patted Meredith's leg. "Do what they tell you and get well."

As they left the room, Aubrey took the hand that wasn't in a sling and squeezed it. "I'm not going anywhere. You're safe. Go to sleep."

* * *

It seemed like only moments later that she was being lifted onto a gurney and wheeled through the halls of the hospital to a private room. She barely stirred. So tired that she didn't even register the instructions they gave her when they tucked her up in her new bed, she said only, "You do it," to Aubrey when they handed her a menu. She was back to sleep in seconds.

Meredith was awakened briefly to have her vitals taken but otherwise slept through until morning. When they carried in her breakfast, she noticed Aubrey heavily asleep in the recliner. "You haven't had anything to eat for a while. If you want to get your strength back, you'll eat this," the nurse said.

On the tray before her were scrambled eggs, bacon, and toast. In a separate bowl was oatmeal. There was also milk and orange juice.

Aubrey awakened. "Breakfast?" he asked.

"I'll never eat all this. It's making me queasy just to smell it."

"That's the concussion," he said. "You need to eat."

She took a piece of toast and nibbled at it. She swallowed some milk.

"When did you last eat?" she asked.

"Lunch yesterday," he confessed.

"Well, if you're going to be my consoler and protector, you'd better get something to eat, too."

"I'll see what they have in the vending machines. Be right back."

She had actually made significant inroads on her eggs by the time he returned with two sandwiches, a Mountain Dew, a candy bar, and a bag of chips.

"Whoa there," she said. "I think you need this bacon."

"No, really," he said. "This looks delicious. Junk food is very nutritious when you're living on your nerves."

She wanted to shake her head, but it was embedded in ice.

"Say," he said. "You know we recovered those photos from Allie's condo. Would you like to look at them? I couldn't see anything, but maybe I missed something."

"Sure. I don't think I can stomach the bacon."

"Well, drink up your juice like a good girl, and I'll hand over the photos. I've been carrying them around in my jacket pocket."

"It's hard to 'look daggers' at someone when you're in this position," she said. "I can't turn my head."

The juice tasted pretty good, but Meredith still had no stomach for the bacon. After Aubrey had eaten his way through his sketchy repast, she said, "Okay. Time for the photos."

"Don't expect much," he said. Taking them out of his jacket pocket, he handed them over to her.

She studied each photo, hungry for some kind of clue. Were these what Allie's dad was looking for? It made more sense that he would be trying to find his letter to be read in case of his death.

"I don't get this obsession with tattoos," she said. "People get them in the weirdest places! Why would someone want one on their shoulder blade?"

Aubrey stopped halfway to the wastebasket. "What? Show me." Pitching his stuff in the basket, he came back over to the bed and looked at the photo.

Meredith didn't understand his interest. It was the shot of all the shirtless men standing around the pool at the resort in the Caymans. The picture was actually focused on one of those cocktails with fruit and umbrellas sticking out of it. The man with the tattoo was in the corner of the picture. The tattoo was perhaps an inch wide.

Agents Marks and Steele entered her room.

"Agents, we've got some evidence here," said Aubrey. Handing Agent Marks the photo, he said, "In the stuff that the Hague sent about Duric, I read up on the mob that he ran around with. They called themselves The Mad Jackals. They were all tattooed on their shoulder blades. They had a photo of one. That," he pointed to the man Meredith had noticed in the photo, "Looks like it could be just like the one I saw. We need to get it enlarged."

"Where did you get the photo?" Agent Steele asked.

"It came from Novak's daughter's apartment. It was with her photos of a trip to the Caymans. I think this is probably her father's back. He's standing right next to the photographer who, going by the other photos, appears to be Allie."

"The other kidnap victim?" asked the woman.

"Yes," answered Agent Marks. "We need to find out if they have such a thing as a magnifying glass in this hospital."

Meredith pressed her call button.

The agents shuffled through the other photos, but there wasn't another showing the man's back.

"Good catch, Meredith," said Aubrey. "If this is what I think it is, it means that for the last twenty-five years, Novak has been masquerading as a Croatian. If he was associated with Duric back then in this paramilitary unit, he is a wanted Serbian war criminal."

"If I could just see his face, I would tell you if he was Allie's father. He's very handsome." Sadness fell over her in spite of Aubrey's jubilation. "Poor Allie. This is going to be terrible for her. Can you imagine having a man like that for a father?"

"Poor Allie, for sure," said Aubrey. "If she survives her kidnapping."

A nurse with a perky pony tail entered the room. Meredith said, "These people are FBI agents who are investigating my kidnapping. We may have found a clue. Do you know where you could find a magnifying glass?"

"They'll have one in the pathology lab," the little woman answered. "I'll send someone down for one."

"Thank you so much," said Meredith. Turning to Aubrey, she said, "Do you know from your reading how tall Duric is?"

"He's a big man. Bully-big. Back in '92, he was six foot three and about 250 pounds."

"The man who kidnapped me was smaller than that, I think. He was in great shape, too. He carried me like I weighed nothing."

"Well, considering that we found you in his backyard, it was probably Novak, or whatever his name is."

"I wonder if he is working with Zoran Duric or is being coerced by him. Duric probably took Allie," she said.

"That's a possibility," said Agent Marks. "Everything is up in the air at the moment."

Aubrey smote his forehead with his hand. "I completely forgot! Meredith doesn't know that my mother escaped!"

"She did? Oh my gosh! How did she do that?"

Aubrey told his mother's story, and her heart lifted. "Oh, you must be so relieved! But the man couldn't have been wearing a mask in public. Did she describe him?"

"She did better than that," said Agent Marks. "She helped our sketch artist draw his likeness." Opening his messenger bag, he removed a copy of the sketch and handed it to her. "Have you seen him?"

Her heart leaped in her chest. Swallowing a lump in her throat, she said, "That's Allie's dad."

"So, he *is* working with Duric. Whether or not he's being coerced, he's guilty of two counts of kidnapping."

At that moment an orderly brought them a magnifying glass. Aubrey took it and thanked the man for his trouble. Putting the photo down on Meredith's table, he held the magnifying glass over it. Meredith noted the little smile that quirked the corner of his mouth.

"Look at that," he said, swinging her bedtable over her lap and handing her the magnifying glass.

The photo looked grainy through the glass, but she could see enough to distinguish a growling beast of some sort. "Well, I'm not real sure what a jackal looks like, but that certainly is a possibility."

He handed the photo and lens to Marks. "That matches the photo the Hague sent me of the tattoos on Duric's men."

Meredith took a deep, satisfied breath. "What a story," she said. "We can use the public's help on this. Can I borrow someone's phone? I want to call Mr. Q."

CHAPTER TWENTY-FIVE

Aubrey could tell the FBI agents weren't totally on board with Meredith making the call to Mr. Q.

"I think we need to discuss this," said Agent Marks. "This news release has international implications."

"We have three kidnappings here," said Meredith, her cheeks flushed. "Has Novak returned to his house? Have your agents caught him? Do they even know where to look?"

Agent Steele answered, "No to all your questions. I would say that engaging the public's help in spotting them would be a huge step forward in the investigation."

Aubrey was surprised by her sudden attitude of confidence.

"Well, you're the boss," said Marks, to Aubrey's surprise.

"I think it would be most effective if we just concentrated on the bare facts of the kidnappings now," said Meredith. "I'm preparing an in-depth story on what we can now call The Mad Jackals to be aired once we've caught these two men. Aubrey and I have hours of taped interviews we took in Sarajevo."

"You sound amazingly sure of yourself," said Marks.

"I'm sure of Aubrey and myself as a team. We're closing in on them. I can feel it. Novak, or whatever his name is, has got to be sweating bullets now that he knows I've escaped."

Meredith made her call to Mr. Q to tell him she had been rescued. She promised him a story for the six o'clock news. "I'll have to clear it with the agents, but I think you should send a production crew out to the safe house. I'm supposed to be resting. It will add some drama to the story to say that I am broadcasting from an undisclosed location."

* * *

The doctor released Meredith during his morning rounds. He gave her warnings about doing too much while she still had a concussion, but she scarcely paid any attention to what he said.

Once they were back at the safe house, she had a teary reunion with Aubrey's mother where they hugged and kissed like long-lost friends. Wasting no time, she amazed him with her resilience by showering, dressing in slacks and a silk shirt, and proceeding to write her story using one hand hunting and pecking on the computer.

The agents had hesitantly okayed the production crew because they didn't think she should be out and about with her injuries.

Meredith was one amazing woman. He thought maybe he had finally found someone who could match his mother in that department. Stana was smitten by her and agreed to appear on the broadcast to describe her ordeal.

Meredith even persuaded him to make a brief appearance as the journalist who had put together all the pieces and rescued her at Novak's house. He agreed on the condition that they omit the piece about his hacking into the law firm.

"You should be good just starting from the property tax angle," she said. "Those are public records."

Aubrey escaped for a while when he was certain that Meredith didn't need him. He went back to the den where they had sat together that day that seemed so far in the past now. Her optimism was shining from her lovely face, but he had no idea how he felt.

They had made a lot of progress, sure. But they still had to catch the bad guys. For all he knew they had hopped a plane and headed off to Vienna together.

But what about Allie? And why had this whole chain of events happened anyway? What was Duric doing in the States? What was his end game? What was the plan he had had in place before the anonymous call had put Meredith and him on the man's trail? The entire situation confounded him, making him more than a little uneasy.

He turned on the gas fireplace and paced around the room. Of course, it was natural that he should worry about Meredith after what she had just been through, wasn't it?

When she had come to consciousness, she had asked for Jan. All the words he had ready to say to her had hidden away inside him once more.

She can't help it, really. Your heart chooses who. And her heart hasn't chosen me.

His dark side began to call the shots. Running his fingers through his hair, he clenched it and pulled until his scalp hurt. He hated his affliction. Why had he ever told Meredith about it? What woman would ever chain herself to him knowing what he was really like?

Suddenly, he had to get outside. He walked through the house to the kitchen and left by the back door. It was midafternoon, and the kids were coming home from school. Just yesterday at this time he was agonizing over whether he would find Meredith. He had. It was a huge blessing. The fact that she hadn't chosen him was just something he was going to have to learn to live with.

He loved his job. There wasn't anywhere he would rather work. But unless she needed his expertise, he didn't need to see Meredith on a regular basis.

Aubrey needed a diversion. What had he been doing before haring off to help her with her story? He had been knee-deep in the sci-fi book he was writing. Could he rebuild his enthusiasm for that project?

A well-groomed Muslim woman in a hijab crossed the road in front of him, holding two small children by their hands. Aubrey stopped where he stood and watched them.

We've completely lost sight of the fact that Duric pathologically hates the Muslims.

Turning around, he hastened back to the safe house and his computer which was now set up in his bedroom due to the confusion downstairs.

He googled Muslim Holy Days. A chart came up. He quickly realized that by the Muslim calendar, it was the beginning of the New Year.

Today was the eighteenth of September. In two days it would be Yom Ashura, the tenth day of Muharram, which was the first month in the Muslim calendar. September twentieth was the Islamic equivalent to Yom Kippur—marking the day that Moses and the Israelites were saved from Pharaoh by the parting of the Red Sea. *For the majority of Shia Muslims, as well as some Sunni Muslims, Ashura marks the climax of the Remembrance of Muharram.*

Aubrey's scalp prickled. Surely there would be commemorative celebrations at the Islamic Community Center in Northbrook.

Not trusting his memory to remember the details, Aubrey carried his open laptop down to the dining room where his colleagues were erecting the set for that evening's newscast about the kidnappings. The backdrop was an evening skyscape of Chicago.

"Aubrey!" said Meredith. "You need to get dressed! At least put on a different shirt. And you need a tie."

"I will in a minute. You need to look at this." He took the computer over to her and showed her what he had found.

"You think that Duric has something planned for that date? It's the day after tomorrow!"

"I know. I'm calling the Imam and telling him to watch the broadcast to see if he recognizes Duric or Novak. They have orientation classes there, remember. Our bad guys may have been in attendance, casing things out."

"Yes! Do it!" urged Meredith. "But then get dressed. We go on air in fifteen minutes!"

"Sorry. Don't have a tie with me."

Agents Steele and Marks were eating in the kitchen. "You need to look at this," he said, laying his laptop before them. The day after tomorrow is a Muslim Holy Day, and the Islamic Community Center is having a celebration."

* * *

Aubrey realized he was totally unprepared for his segment on the news. As he pulled on a clean shirt, he went over the details in his mind that had led him to find Meredith. He had just a few minutes to jot them down in order before he ran downstairs for the broadcast.

Meredith, whose head surely must be pounding, sat at the dining room table in front of the screen of the Chicago skyline. Studio lights were set up, and various members of the production team were stationed about the room along with the FBI agents, Marks, and Steele. Hers was the opening story.

> *Good Evening. I'm Meredith Montgomery, coming to you live tonight from an undisclosed FBI safe house in Chicagoland. Tonight, I will give you an account of my recent kidnapping by a Bosnian-Serb War Criminal wanted for the commission of war crimes twenty-five years ago. This man [cut to drawing of Novak's face] going by the alias of Mikal Novak, was a member of The Mad Jackals, a paramilitary group which committed atrocities against the Bosnian Muslims during the years 1992 through 1995 when the Dayton Peace Accords were signed. He was my kidnapper.*
>
> *Novak is known to be connected to Zoran Duric, the leader of the Mad Jackals, who has recently been sighted in Chicago. [cut to picture of Duric], There have been two other recent kidnappings which are believed to have been orchestrated by Duric—those of Alexandra Novak, a veterinarian in Evanston, who is the daughter of Mikal Novak, and Stana Kettering, formerly of Bosnia, who lives in Hyde Park.*
>
> *Fortunately, Ms. Kettering escaped, and is here to give us an account of her kidnapping.*
>
> *[cut to Stana Kettering who gives her statement about her kidnapping by Novak]*
>
> *I was kidnapped during my investigation from the scene of Alexandra Novak's abduction at her apartment in Evanston. The FBI agent who accompanied me at the time was shot, and remains hospitalized in critical condition. I was fortunate to be rescued yesterday from Novak's property in Lake Forest by my colleague, Aubrey Kettering, and the FBI. Here to report on the chain of evidence he uncovered, is Mr. Aubrey Kettering, who also happens to be Stana Kettering's son:*

[cut to Aubrey giving his summary of the path of his investigation from finding the property tax records to finding Novak's gardening shed]

The genesis of all these crimes and hatreds goes back many centuries culminating in the Bosnian War, where Croatians, Muslims, and Serbs, all of whom were also Bosnians, erupted into a brutal war. After the peace was signed in 1995, many Bosnian Muslims immigrated to Northbrook Chicago, where they have built a mosque. Bosnian Serbs and Croats immigrated to already established settlements on the south side of Chicago.

We ask any of you who may have seen either of these men [cut to split screen with both men] to telephone WOOT's tipline or the FBI. [cut to graphic of telephone numbers].

Now we will return to WOOT's downtown studio for other news.

At the conclusion of the broadcast, Aubrey watched as Meredith slumped in her chair. He went to her and helped her up.

"Well done, but you've got to go lie down. Even heroines gotta rest sometimes."

"But what are we going to do about the Community Center?"

"I just left a message for the Imam that it was extremely important that he watch our news coverage tonight. I'll try to get in touch with him now. Let's go to that little den. You can lie down and listen while I make my call. I'll put it on speaker."

The Imam was extremely glad Aubrey called. "I am sorry for the difficulties you mother and your colleague have had. I think I recognize one of those men. The one in the drawing has been attending our Orientation to Islam program for months. I have always had the impression that his background was Croatian. I realize now, with the more recent picture, that I have seen Duric somewhere. His eyes and long nose are familiar. But, at the moment, I can't recall where I've seen him. It may have been Bosnia."

"Would you object to having the FBI come to the Center tomorrow to sweep for bombs or anything else suspicious? We understand that you have an important celebration taking place there on Thursday. We will, of course, send copies of the pictures to your local police."

"Of course. We would be most grateful. These men are dangerous."

"Duric, in particular," said Aubrey. "Please try to remember where it is you have seen him."

Aubrey hung up and turned to Meredith. All the animation that had been there during her broadcast had evaporated, and her complexion was gray.

"You look like you're in pain, honey. It's been over twenty-four hours. You can take those pain meds now."

"Maybe I'll just take one," she said softly. "You need to talk to the agents. They need to know about the Islamic holiday. Where have they gone?"

"I told them already. They are briefing their relief agents, Murphy and Casson, who will be here tonight."

Marks entered the den. "Let's plan to go to the Center the next day with bomb dogs and go over the place. We'll put two sets of agents there to guard the entrances."

"Sounds good to me," said Aubrey.

"You're on the right track. We finished our investigation of the Novak property. There was bomb-making equipment in the garage. Now you've given us a target."

After Marks left, Aubrey was unable to resist pulling a chair up to the side of the couch where Meredith lay. He stroked the hair on the other side of her head from her injury. "Where are your meds? I'll bring them to you."

CHAPTER TWENTY-SIX

Dinner with his parents was a stressful meal. None of them had any doubt that the Islamic Center was the target. As the coffee was being poured, Aubrey's dad said, "Duric has been very careful to remain in the background. Do you think it's possible that Novak is the moving force here? He could have hired Duric to come here from Vienna and arrange the bombing."

"But what about Allie's kidnapping?" asked Aubrey.

"Has it occurred to you that the whole thing might have been staged? Maybe her father sent her somewhere safe," said his dad.

"But there was evidence at the scene that showed her door had been jimmied open and she had been dragged out of the house," said Aubrey.

"Could have been staged," said his dad.

"But she just up and left her clinic," said Aubrey.

"Maybe her father told Allie her life was at stake."

"Those two men do seem to be working together. Novak's was the forwarding address for Duric's property taxes."

"And Novak kidnapped your mother for Duric. Don't forget that," said his dad.

"How is Meredith holding up?" asked Stana.

"She's overdone it with that broadcast, though she probably wouldn't have missed it for the world. She's finally took something for the pain and is sound asleep."

"She's one tough cookie with all she's been through," said his dad. "Reminds me of your mother."

"Funny," said Aubrey. "I was thinking of that, too."

* * *

Along with Special Agents Marks and Steele, Aubrey and Meredith met the Imam at the Center the next morning. They were accompanied by the bomb detection squad and their dogs as well as the local police.

The old man was clearly rattled. "I don't know if I should call off the celebration tomorrow," he said.

Marks spoke. "Aubrey here has told us you have had this fellow who calls himself Novak attending your orientations. He's been posing as a Croatian, but he's actually a Bosnian Serb who belonged to a particularly nasty Serbian terrorist group led by Zoran Duric. They are both in the area, as you heard on the news. There is a good chance you are being targeted during the celebrations tomorrow. We found the bomb-making materials in Novak's garage.

"We have bomb-sniffing dogs who can go through your Center today and tomorrow morning. How many do you expect at the celebration?"

"About two hundred. It's on a weekday, or there would be more."

Agent Steele spoke. "We should be able to evacuate that many in a very short time if needed. You have adequate exits here."

"Do you heat with natural gas or electricity?" asked Aubrey.

"Gas," said the Imam.

"Good thinking, Aubrey. That gives us a good idea that the terrorist will target the gas line somewhere. We should probably have the gas company out today to mark where the line enters the building from outside, as well as the inside," said Agent Marks."

Agent Steele took out her phone and went a short way away to take care of this.

Aubrey said, "Perhaps you could give us a tour, so we know what we're dealing with."

"Certainly. I'd be happy to. Where we are meeting now is obviously the office wing. I will take you to the mosque."

He led the way to the big, empty, modern domed room. "The minaret is accessed by an interior staircase over there," he pointed.

"There isn't much space to secrete a bomb here," said Meredith. "The minaret would be a good symbolic spot, but it wouldn't lead to much loss of life."

The Imam looked pained. "And loss of life, Muslim lives, is what these men specialize in."

"Yes," said Meredith. "I'm sorry to be so blunt, but it is what it is."

Nodding, he led the way out of the room. This separate wing is the instructional area. We clear away the tables and chairs when we have a celebration. Back there in the corner is the kitchen. We have a gas stove."

"I think we can count that out. It would be certain to be seen," said Agent Steele.

"Where is your furnace room?" asked Marks. "And your maintenance cupboard?"

"Back here." The Imam led the way back down the hall toward the offices.

"Do you have a full-time janitor?" asked Meredith.

"Yes."

"And how long has he been with you?" she asked.

"For years. Come I will introduce you. He will be doing the glass doors at the front. They have to be cleaned every day."

The janitor was heavily bearded with a dark green overall which hung loosely on his spare frame.

"Hamid, these people are here because there is a threat to the Center. We'd like to look in the furnace room and the maintenance room."

The man gave a short bow of the head. "Come, I will show you."

The janitor led them to two small dark areas. There was no evidence of bombs. "We'll have the dogs in here," said Agent Marks.

Meredith introduced herself and asked, "Has anyone been here to service the furnace lately?"

"Yes," Hamid said. "He came yesterday. He said everything was working fine."

The Imam's composure evaporated. "What did this man look like?"

"He had a full beard with some gray in it. Balding on top. Brown eyes. He was very large."

"Did he have an appointment?" asked the Imam.

"No. He just showed up. He said it was a regular maintenance check. I didn't realize it was time for another one. He wasn't too talkative. I think he was from our part of the world. He had a heavy accent."

Aubrey's eyes met Meredith's. "I think we've found our bomber."

* * *

The dogs searched the furnace room, the maintenance room, and the entire route of the gas line as indicated by the gas company. They found nothing.

"That only means he's coming tonight or early tomorrow morning," said Aubrey. "I'm bringing my sleeping bag and spending the night nearby."

"That's unnecessary," said Agent Marks. "We are fully capable of handling this from this point."

"Yeah," Aubrey said. "I know. But I need to get the story."

Meredith grinned. "Me, too."

"Neither of you is going to be here," said Agent Steele firmly. "You could compromise the investigation. That's final. We'll have agents on guard here overnight if that is acceptable to the Imam."

The man nodded, his lips a thin line.

"Well, you can't keep us from coming to the celebration," said Aubrey.

Meredith nodded. "Where would any of us be in this investigation if it weren't for Aubrey?" she asked.

When the agents left, Aubrey told the Imam. "We'll be here at seven a.m. Will there be someone to let us in?"

The holy man said, "I will be. I intend to spend the night on the pull-out bed in my office, and of course Khalid will be with me."

* * *

That evening at the safe house, Meredith was glad she was finally able to eat, her nausea having subsided. Stana had used all her pent-up frustration at being "cooped up" to make a turkey dinner for the family and the agents protecting them. She insisted they all eat together.

Meredith found out where Aubrey got his cooking skills. In addition to turkey, they had cranberry stuffing, sweet potatoes in orange shells, white potatoes and gravy, green beans with almonds, and an apple pie for dessert.

"Rushing the season a bit, Mom," said Aubrey, "But I don't mind."

Meredith and Stana weren't allowed to clean up but were sent to the den where they both collapsed on the comfortable couch.

"How is your head?" Aubrey's mom asked her.

"I'm thinking of taking another pain pill. I want to be able to sleep. I think tomorrow will be a big day."

"I think that's a good idea. Tell me where you put them."

Stana fetched her pills and brought her some water. After she had taken them, she said, "Your family has been so good to me. Thank you."

"As my husband would say, we want you to last."

"I'm sure you're wondering about Aubrey and me," Meredith said in a low voice.

"Not really. It's obvious that you care about one another, but Aubrey hasn't said anything."

"You should probably know that the man I loved was brutally murdered in the Middle East just a couple of months ago. I'm kind of emotionally unavailable right now."

Stana looked at Meredith, her eyes solemn. "I'm so sorry to hear that. You know, I wasn't exactly emotionally available, as you put it, when my husband came along. I was highly traumatized in the middle of a war. But he was strong and patient. These things have a way of working out if they are supposed to."

"I don't know if I can risk ever caring for someone as much as I cared for Jan. The whole idea terrifies me," Meredith said.

"The heart has a mind of its own," Stana said. "Or at least mine does. I thought I never wanted or needed a man in my life after what I had been through. But I was wrong."

"I must admit, life seems pretty arid without love," Meredith replied. "I love my work, but I can see already that it would make for a pretty stark life. I see so much tragedy."

"That's how it was in the war," said Stana. "Then my husband came along. At first, the light inside of me was just a little one—more like the possibility of light."

Meredith bit her lip, giving the matter some thought. "Yes. I can understand that. I feel that way when Aubrey's hair stands up a certain way because he's concentrating, and he's been running his hands through it. I feel that way when we're working, and it seems like our minds sort of meld together. It's like one of us picks up where the other leaves off."

"Exactly. And not to embarrass you, but I can tell you are physically attracted to each other," Stana said.

"Yes," she said. "But I don't think I should let that cloud my thinking."

Stana gave a small chuckle. "It's not everything, true. But it's a start."

Aubrey entered the room. He looked from one of them to the other. "Should my ears be burning?" he asked.

Stana laughed. "Come join us. I was just telling Meredith about meeting your father."

CHAPTER TWENTY-SEVEN

Aubrey woke up in the night with the feeling that something was wrong. The time was four a.m. They had missed something. Duric was too crafty to fall into their hands so easily. Something was telling him that he needed to get to the Cultural Center.

Getting out of bed, he dressed quickly in dark clothes. He stuck his Glock into the back of his waistband and put on his black leather jacket.

As he tried to sneak out of the house, he was stopped by Agent Murphy who was keeping watch over the safe house.

"Where are you going?"

Aubrey said, "To the Islamic Cultural Center. Something isn't right. Don't worry. There are agents guarding the place, so I won't be alone."

"Just let me call to tell them you're on your way," said the agent.

Aubrey waited with growing impatience. Finally, Agent Murphy rejoined him and said, "I have to come with you. You've forgotten. You have no car. We'll take the agency's. You'll have to give me directions."

"Okay. I'm calling the Imam to tell him we're coming."

* * *

Aubrey was glad there was a full moon. It would make it much easier to see.

"Where are the agents?" he asked Murphy.

"They're inside, hidden close to all the entrances."

"Something is telling me that our man is too smart just to walk in. Let's walk around the perimeter," said Aubrey.

There wasn't much to see on the ground, because there weren't many hiding places. Aubrey concentrated on the roof. Duric might try to get in through a vent. At some earlier date, he and Novak had probably scoped the place out completely.

Then, silhouetted in the moonlight, he saw a figure rappelling up the side of the minaret to the prayer balcony. Nudging Murphy, he pointed.

Aubrey whispered, "There's a stairway going down inside the minaret. We've got to get in."

"I'll call the agent near the back door."

No one answered Murphy's call.

"Something's wrong."

"I'll call the Imam," said Aubrey.

No one answered that call either.

"We're too late," said Aubrey. "Someone's already inside and has gotten to all of them. We'll have to follow that guy up the rope. Have you ever rappelled?"

"No," said Murphy.

"It takes some skill. I'll go. You call for backup."

Aubrey prayed the climber hadn't pulled the rope up after himself. Running around the building, he finally located the place where the end of the rope was hidden behind some bushes. They must be planning to leave this way, or they would have pulled the rope up.

He wished he had his climbing gloves and boots. His shoes were too slick-soled. Pausing to take off his socks and shoes, he finally grasped the rope and began his climb barefoot. Fortunately, the night was not too cold.

It had been too long since he'd done this. However, the skill came back to him as he climbed the way he had learned on trips to the Rocky Mountains when he was a boy.

The bricks felt rough under his uncalloused feet, and by the time he got to the balcony, they were bleeding. Using the well-anchored rope, he managed to pull himself over the small balcony and onto the prayer platform. The door to the stairwell was opened. Taking out his Glock, he held it ready as he peered down the stairwell. He saw no one, but it was dark. Inching down the stairs with his arms fully extended and his hands holding his gun, he made it to the ground floor of the Center.

Aubrey paused to listen. He heard nothing. Flattening himself against the wall of the mosque, he tried to orient himself and remember which way the furnace room was. The minaret was on the east. He vaguely recalled that the furnace room was on the north side of the building through the hallway that branched off the office wing.

He began moving through the mosque, toward the office wing, staying close to the wall. Once he found the right hallway, he could see a moving light down at the end. *Flashlight.*

He crept, still flush with the wall. There were probably two of them in here, he had to remember. In the darkness, his feet encountered something soft, but solid. A body! He stepped over it silently. Aubrey sincerely hoped the man wasn't dead and realized it was actually a blessing he was barefoot.

When he reached the furnace room, he heard the hushed tones of Serbo-Croatian, as two men conversed. Aubrey listened.

From what he could tell, they were making a small hole in the gas line leading to the heating system. Clever. It would leak until it filled the air of the Cultural Center and Mosque, and by the morning the atmosphere would be full of it, vastly increasing the explosive power of a bomb. Where was the bomb itself going to be placed?

Hoping to hear, he edged closer. He must have made a noise for one of the men said, "There's someone else outside. Go!"

As the man exited the room, Aubrey had no recourse but to fire his Glock. The sound echoed through the corridors, and the man fell forward.

He was followed closely by his colleague who used his flashlight to blind Aubrey. He heard a sneezing sound and bullet hit him in the chest like a freight train. He went down. Writhing in pain, he heard the shooter running down the hallway. Just before he passed out, he heard the clatter of one of the glass entry doors as the man escaped.

* * *

When he came to, all the lights were on, and an EMT was leaning over him. He had no idea how much time had passed.

"One of them got away," he breathed out. "And the gas line has been ruptured in there. There's a bomb somewhere."

"You've lost a lot of blood," the EMT said. "Try to be calm." He turned to the man next to him. "Go for one of the FBI guys. Tell him this one is awake. Something about a bomb."

Aubrey struggled to sit up but was forced down. "What time is it?"

"It's six in the morning, and this place is crawling with FBI. Don't worry."

His chest hurt like the devil. He passed out again.

The next time he came to they were using the defibrillation paddles on him. Aubrey realized his heart had stopped.

He *had* to live!

"My phone," he mumbled. "In my pocket."

The EMT brought it out, but said, "We just resuscitated you. You're not calling anyone. I'll do it."

"Marks," he said. "Speaker."

"We're almost to the hospital."

"Important."

Marks came on the line.

"Ruptured the gas line," Aubrey managed to say. "Bomb planted somewhere."

"We got it. Trying to defuse it now. The guy you shot was Novak. Was Duric with him?"

"Yeah."

"He got away. He must have a wireless detonator. We have a BOLO out for him."

He realized they were working on a live bomb that could go off any time Duric pressed his detonator. "Throw the bomb away! Are you crazy?"

"We've almost got it."

The ambulance doors opened, and they wheeled him into the hospital. Marks had hung up.

CHAPTER TWENTY-EIGHT

Meredith knew something was wrong. Aubrey was gone and so was Agent Murphy. His partner, Agent Casson, said that they had gone to the Islamic Center around four a.m. She had heard nothing from him. It was now seven, and they were supposed to be leaving for the Center together.

Agent Marks's and Agent Steele's phones were going to voicemail. So was Aubrey's. Going to her bedroom she called for a taxi and then sneaked out the back door, so Agent Casson could not stop her. She told the cabbie to take her to Northbrook and the Center. In a state of high anxiety, she fiddled with her sling as she drove. Her head still pounded, and her shoulder pain was almost unendurable.

When she arrived, she found the Center alive with flashing lights and crowds of spectators. Several TV vans were there, including WOOT's. She couldn't even get close to the Center. Never had she been so frustrated. Was Aubrey all right?

Finally, she made her way to the WOOT van and talked to her colleague, Jenny Fredericks.

"What is going on? I was supposed to be in there, and now I can't even get near! Aubrey's in there!"

"No, he isn't," she said. "Just when we pulled in they were taking him away in an ambulance."

All idea of her story left Meredith's head.

Aubrey! Hospital!

She called for another taxi, telling them she would be waiting on the next street.

What did you do, you crazy man? Why didn't you wake me up to go with you?

As soon as the taxi arrived, she told the cabbie to take her to the nearest hospital.

* * *

Aubrey was in surgery. That was the only thing she could find out. She didn't know what had happened and she didn't know how serious it was.

The news was on NBC local news in the waiting room. Forcing herself to focus, she listened.

> *The FBI is searching for this man, Zoran Duric. [Photo of Zoran Duric] He and his partner, who has been identified as Mikal Novak ruptured a gas line in the Islamic Cultural Center in Northbrook where they also planted bombs. Fortunately, with the use of bomb dogs, the FBI located several behind vents inside the Center. They were disarmed without any injuries. The process was a dangerous one, as the bomb could have exploded at any moment. Today was to have been the celebration of the Islamic holiday Yom Ashura. Duric is a fugitive who is armed and extremely dangerous. Call the FBI or the Chicago Police if you see him. [cut to phone numbers]*
>
> *The FBI has told us that the plot to blow up the center was foiled by the brave actions of WOOT TV analyst, Aubrey Kettering, who scaled the minaret outside the center in pursuit of a man he saw entering. When he caught this man and his partner in the furnace room, he was able to shoot one of them, but then was wounded himself. Mr. Kettering was taken to Northwestern Memorial in critical condition.*
>
> *We will, of course, keep you informed of any recent developments in this story as it unfolds.*

Critical condition. Aubrey.

I can't lose him.

At that moment, she became aware of a man in a green coverall entering the ER. It was Zoran Duric. And she didn't have a gun. She didn't even have pepper spray. There wasn't a security officer in sight.

She watched as Duric pulled a gun on the nurse at the ER desk and demanded to see Aubrey Kettering. With his other hand, he held out what looked like a detonator.

"I will blow up this hospital with just one press of my thumb if you do not take me to him."

The nurse looked him straight in the eye. "You cannot see Mr. Kettering. He is in surgery."

Meredith walked stealthily up behind Duric. The nurse kept her eyes trained on the man and did not give her away. Drawing back her foot, Meredith kicked him solidly behind his knee, and he went down in a heap. Cursing her sling, she managed to straddle him and using two fingers on her good hand, poked hard at his eyes, just as he was aiming his gun. He screamed and dropped it. Moving as quickly as she could, she grasped the gun and held it to his temple. "If you move an inch, I will shoot!" She shouted, "Call security! This man is a murderer!"

"I'll detonate the bomb!" he shouted back.

"No, you won't. It's already been defused. You've failed."

The man howled, rubbing his bleeding eyes. "Zoran Duric, you are going to go to prison for the rest of your lousy life!" She brought the gun down hard on the bridge of his nose. "That was for Aubrey!" She whacked him in the temple. "That was for almost killing us in Bosnia!"

He struggled to grab the gun from her, but she held it out of his reach. At that moment, a security officer came running in.

"This is the man who tried to blow up the Islamic Cultural Center this morning," she said, her voice hard. "He is Zoran Duric, a war criminal, and he shot a man who is in surgery here." She struck Duric on the cheekbone.

The security officer spoke into the radio clipped to his shoulder, "Assistance needed ASAP in the ER. We have the man in the BOLO."

By the time help had arrived, she was so enraged they had to pull her off of him.

* * *

Meredith was very happy to see Special Agents Steele and Marks when they strode into the security office at the hospital, followed by a contingent of agents who took over from the hospital security team, taking Zoran Duric into custody.

"Good work, Meredith. I suppose he came here in search of Aubrey? How is he doing?"

"He's in surgery. What of Novak?"

"He didn't make it. Aubrey shot him right in the heart," Agent Marks said. "Better than living in a Federal Penitentiary."

Meredith gave a heavy sigh. "Poor Allie. What a shock this is going to be. She'll probably hear about it on the news, wherever she is. I suppose we'll never even know his true name." She turned to Agent Steele. "Could you do me a favor and call Stana and Dr. Kettering? I don't have their number, and they might not know anything. When I left this morning, they weren't even up."

Agent Steele agreed to this task, while Agent Marks filled her in on what had happened at the Center that morning.

"Novak and Duric used silencers to shoot our agents. Two of them didn't make it."

"What about the Imam?" she asked.

"I'm afraid the poor man was a martyr for his beliefs. They killed him and his bodyguard, too."

Meredith covered her eyes with her hands, and the tears that were lurking finally loosed and she let out a muffled sob. "Will the hate never end?"

"I haven't had a chance to tell you yet," said Agent Marks, "But with DNA taken from his home, we have matched Novak's DNA to the seal of the envelope your death threat came in. It looks like he was the one behind your stalking, not Duric."

"That doesn't make any sense!" she said, startled.

"Did you ever speak to Allie about what you were doing?"

Meredith remembered their dinner together at O'Henry's. How long ago it seemed!

"Yes. I asked for her help. I wanted her to talk to her father about Duric after I got that anonymous call. She said he never talked about the war. But she must have said something to him. That's got to be what put them on our trail." She wiped her eyes with her sleeve. "What a horrible mess this is!"

"Novak had been going to that Cultural Center for months," said Agent Marks. "I think he must have brought Duric over here to do the bombing. It looks like Novak was the instigator, not Duric. Pretty scary to think of that guy living among us all these years, nursing that hatred as more and more Bosnian Muslims moved to Northbrook."

"Quite a story," said Meredith. "I only hope Aubrey doesn't have to pay for it with his life."

After the agents left to take Duric away, she sat down in the security office and stared at the wall. Finally, pulling out her phone, she called Mr. Q.

"I just took down Duric, and the FBI has taken him away," she said. "Aubrey is in surgery. They won't tell me anything further than that."

* * *

Meredith was deeply grateful when the stunned Stana and Dr. Kettering showed up in the ER.

"I'm so sorry," she said to them. "Aubrey left the house in the middle of the night without anyone knowing except the FBI guys. One of them went with him to the Center."

Meredith hugged Stana, and said, "Now that you're here maybe we can find out something. They won't tell me anything because I'm not family. All I know is that he's in surgery."

Aubrey's mother and father approached the ER intake nurse. Meredith couldn't hear their conversation, but shortly they rejoined her.

"He's in surgery. He was resuscitated twice." The woman wet her lips and then bit the lower one, and Meredith could see she was trying not to cry. "It's really bad. I'm afraid I can't take it in."

"Can you at least go up to the surgery waiting room?" Meredith asked.

"Yes. We'd like you to come with us."

Meredith followed the Ketterings to the elevator. They went up to the surgery floor and stepped out into a crowded waiting room. The news of the Islamic Center shootings was now on CNN, and everyone in the room was glued to the TV.

Meredith's phone rang. It was a call from the Caymans. She stepped out into the hall.

"Hello?"

"Meredith, it's Allie. I had a terrible time getting your new number. I finally called your mother. Is it true, what I'm seeing on the news? Aubrey shot my father? He's dead?"

"It is. I'm afraid so, Allie. I'm sorry. He was mixed up in the whole thing at the Muslim center. There was a bomb. The FBI just defused it."

She heard a sharp intake of breath, but it didn't sound like Allie was crying.

"You're in the Caymans? We thought you were kidnapped!"

"My father told me to leave town and not to tell anyone. He said I was in danger from someone from his past in Bosnia."

"Allie, I'm not sure what you've heard, but your father was Serbian. He's been living under an assumed identity all these years."

Silence.

"Actually, I knew. He didn't know that I knew, though."

Meredith's stomach clenched. "How did you find out?"

"I knew he wasn't a good man. He never hurt me, but he was violent with the poor people who worked for us. I began to wonder about his past. When I was in Europe, I went to the Hague a few years ago and looked at the pictures of wanted criminals from the war. I saw his photo. He was called Drasko Subotic."

So, Aubrey was right, after all. "Go on," said Meredith.

"There was a note with the photo saying he was dead. I have been so full of guilt for so many years, Meredith. I just couldn't turn him in. He was my father."

"I'm so sorry, Allie," she managed to say. "When will you be coming home?"

"I think I'll stay down here for a while. I have a lot to process. How is Aubrey?"

"We're waiting to hear. I'm sorry you've had such a shock. This whole thing has been horrible."

"It wasn't that much of a surprise," her friend said. "I knew something was going on. I didn't want to face it."

Meredith struggled against her feeling of betrayal. "I'll be here for you when you get back," she said finally.

"Thanks, Meredith. That says a lot, considering my dad kidnapped you. I . . . I can't believe I'm even saying this. I can't believe all this really happened. I hope Aubrey makes it."

"Thanks. I've got to go now to see if they've heard anything. Bye, Allie."

* * *

"I can't stand this," said Stana, burying her face in her husband's chest as he curled an arm around her.

"It's my fault," said Meredith. Guilt was eating her alive. "I talked him into working with me on this story, and when he found out it was about Bosnia, he was all in."

"You aren't responsible for Aubrey's decisions," said the professor. "He's always been like that about his enthusiasms."

"It's the Slav in him, Meredith," said his mother. "He's very passionate."

A doctor came out to talk to a waiting family who left afterward for the recovery room, freeing up their chairs in the corner. As Stana and Meredith sat down, the professor volunteered to go for coffee.

"I'll just have a Coke," said Meredith.

The wait was long. Stana spent the time telling them stories about Aubrey.

Meredith felt such pain in her chest she thought her heart was physically breaking. She couldn't even imagine Stana's pain. And all the stories she was telling were just making Meredith feel worse.

Aubrey was so alive. Such a force for good in the world. She wasn't ready to let go. Somehow, he had stolen her heart, and she hadn't even realized it.

She couldn't stand listening to Stana's remembrances for another instant. She felt like she was going to jump out of her skin. Leaping up from her chair, she said, "I had better go call my mother. Maybe she's seen the news. Maybe she's put it all together and knows that I'm involved."

The call to her mother did not go well. She was terribly worried and insisted that she visit Meredith on her way home from Michigan to Atlanta.

"I'm not in a good place emotionally right now, Mom," she said. "The man who is critically injured? The one who is in surgery right now? I think I've fallen in love with him. I'm a mess. I don't know if he's going to live or not. I don't want you to see me like this."

"Oh, sweetie! You haven't even had a chance to get over Jan! I'm so sorry you are going through this. Do you think maybe you need to come home for a while?"

"Maybe I'll go up to the UP. No. That reminds me too much of Jan and Dad. I guess you really can't run away from grief."

Her mother said, "I'm flying to Chicago tomorrow. I'll make my own way to your condo. Don't worry about me. Do you still keep your key in the same hiding place?"

"Yes."

"I'll find plenty to do. I've been itching to decorate my guest bedroom."

Some of the pain in Meredith's breast loosened. She guessed you were really never too old to need your mother.

"Thanks, Mom. But I may be at the hospital."

"That's all right. You do what you need to do. I just want to be on hand if you need me."

"I love you, Mom."

"I love you, too, sweetie. More than tongue can tell."

When Meredith got back to the waiting room, there was news. Stana was beaming. "We just got a status report! A nurse came out to tell us that they finally have Aubrey stabilized. Now it's just a matter of doing the repairs. She said she couldn't tell us how long it's going to be, but it will be at least a couple of hours."

Meredith sank into her chair, realizing that she was shaking all over. "Oh, Stana. Oh, Stana, that's wonderful news!" She put her head in her hands and wept.

* * *

When Aubrey came out of surgery, he went into Cardiac Intensive Care. Meredith wasn't family, so she couldn't visit him, and Stana and Dr. Kettering were only allowed to stay for ten minutes.

When they came out after their first visit, Aubrey's mother squeezed Meredith's hands and said, "It's a miracle. He's going to be fine, honey. He just needs to mend. He knows you're here and that you can't come in. He says, 'Go home and work on the story.'"

Meredith smiled for the first time in what seemed like days.

EPILOGUE

Meredith stayed at the safe house that night, only because she was too tired and weak to pack up and go home. When she woke up the next morning, the cleaners were there.

She showered quickly, dressed in jeans and her Northwestern sweatshirt, put on her sling, and packed up. On the way home to Evanston, she stopped at IHOP for breakfast, treating herself to pumpkin pancakes.

Life could not be sweeter. Aubrey had had a good night, and if things continued as they were going, she would be able to see him in a couple of days. And she could use that time. She had a heck of a story to write.

Stopping at her florist in Evanston, she ordered a Star Wars balloon bouquet to be delivered to Northwestern Memorial with a card attached that said, "Get better at warp speed. All my love, Meredith."

Her breast was filled with cheer and light, and she wondered how long it would be before her mother arrived. When she got to the condo, she tried to unlock the door, but it was already open.

Moving inside, she called, "Mother?"

She heard footsteps coming through from her family room. A figure stood before her, silhouetted against the morning light coming in through the sheers in the dining room.

"Hello, darling."

Standing before her, smoking his pipe, was Jan.

The End

THE STORY BEHIND THE STORY

As you can tell from this novel, Meredith and Aubrey at not the only ones with a passion for Balkan history. In both graduate and undergraduate school, I majored in Eastern European history, politics, and economics. Surprisingly, with such a specific major, I was able to find just the job for me.

In the mid-'90's I worked for the University of Dayton as Assistant in Charge of International Programs. In those days, so shortly after the Bosnian War's peace was negotiated in at Wright-Patterson air force base in Dayton, all our International Programs focused on Bosnia. Under the guidance of the Director, I planned an anniversary celebration of the signing of the Dayton Peace Accords. It included the heads of state in Bosnia and several United States dignitaries as well as the celebrated Sarajevo Circle. The latter was a band made up of musicians from each of the Bosnian minorities—Serbs, Croats, and Muslims. The celebration was a major event attended by people from all over the US and Bosnia.

My other duties included writing grants for restoration projects like the Sarajevo Art museum, writing White Papers about War Criminals, applying on behalf of the university to host Bosnian college students and a myriad of other duties concerning Bosnia.

I met many people from all walks of life who had suffered in the war. It was an intense education about a situation very few Americans understood. In this novel, I have tried to submerge the reader in matters which still simmer in that country, even twenty-five years later.

Zoran Duric and Drasko Zubotic are figments of my imagination.

OTHER BOOKS BY G.G. VANDAGRIFF

ROMANTIC SUSPENSE

Breaking News
Sleeping Secrets
Balkan Echo

REGENCY ROMANCE

His Mysterious Lady
Her Fateful Debut
Not an Ordinary Baronet
Love Unexpected
*
Lord Grenville's Choice
Lord John's Dilemma
Lord Basingstoke's Downfall
*
The Duke's Undoing
The Taming of Lady Kate
Miss Braithwaite's Secret
Rescuing Rosalind

Lord Trowbridge's Angel
The Baron and the Bluestocking
*
Much Ado about Lavender
Spring in Hyde Park (anthology)

HISTORICAL NOVELS

The Last Waltz: A Novel of Love and War
Exile
Defiance

WOMEN'S FICTION

The Only Way to Paradise
Pieces of Paris

GENEALOGICAL MYSTERIES

Cankered Roots
Of Deadly Descent
Tangled Roots
Poisoned Pedigree
The Hidden Branch

NON-FICTION

Deliverance from Depression

Voices In Your Blood

ABOUT THE AUTHOR

I realize that I am one of those rare people in the world who gets to live a life full of passion, suspense, angst, fulfillment, humor, and mystery. I am a writer. Every day when I sit down to my computer, I enter into a world of my own making. I am in the head of a panoply of characters ranging from a nineteen-year-old Austrian debutante (The Last Waltz) to a raging psychopath (The Arthurian Omen). Then there are the sassy heroines of my Regency romances . . .

How did this come about? I think I was wired to be a writer when I was born. There were a lot of things about my surroundings that I couldn't control during my growing up years, so I retreated to whatever alternate existence I was creating. The habit stuck, and now my family finds themselves living in my current reality during dinnertime as I overflow with enthusiasm about Wales, Austria, Italy, Regency England, or World War II. My latest craze is Bosnia.

Formerly a traditionally published, award-winning author, I went Indie in 2012. In that time I have become an Amazon #1 best-selling author of Regency romances. I enjoy genre-hopping, having published a genealogical mystery series, two women's fiction novels, three historical romances, three romantic suspense novels, thirteen Regency romances, some novellas, and a couple of non-fiction offerings.

With a BA from Stanford and an MA from George Washington University in International Relations, I somehow stumbled into finance. But, once my husband was through law school, I never wanted to do anything but write and raise kids. Now the kids are gone, but (even better) there are seven grandchildren who provide my rewards for finishing a manuscript.

Aside from the grandchildren, my favorite things include: Florence, Italy; snow storms; the Chicago Cubs; Oreos; real hot chocolate; Sundance Resort; lilacs; and dachshunds.

You can visit my website at ggvandagriff.com, follow me on Facebook or check out my Author Page on Facebook. Also, please follow me on Bookbub!

G.G. Vandagriff
Visit my website at www.ggvandagriff.com

Printed in the United States of America

First Printing: December 2018
OW Press